CHANGELING

Melissa Diem lives in Dublin with her partner, Peter, and daughters Jessica, Melanie and Saoirse. Her youngest daughter, Saoirse, is profoundly disabled and suffers from intractable epilepsy. Melissa is currently working on her second novel and studying Psychology at Trinity College Dublin.

CHANGELING

MELISSA DIEM

TiVOLi

Tivoli
an imprint of Gill & Macmillan Ltd
Hume Avenue
Park West
Dublin 12
with associated companies throughout the world

www.gillmacmillan.ie

© Melissa Diem 2004
0 7171 3730 9

Print origination by Carole Lynch
Printed by AIT Nørhaven A/S, Denmark

*The paper used in this book is made from the wood pulp of
managed forests. For every tree felled, at least one tree is
planted, thereby renewing natural resources.*

A catalogue record is available for this book
from the British Library.

1 3 5 4 2

This book is a work of fiction. Names, characters, places and
incidents are either the product of the author's imagination or
are used fictiously. Any resemblance to actual events or locales
or persons, living or dead, is entirely coincidental.

Dedication

For Peter, Jessica and Melanie
my travelling companions,
and
for Saoirse,
who brought us to unexpected and
remarkable new worlds

Acknowledgments

To my partner, Peter, who felt each word as I did, and my daughters, Jessica, Melanie and Saoirse. My extraordinary family inspire and support me daily.

To my sister Adrienne, a kindred spirit who supports me in everything I do, regardless of how ridiculous it may be.

I am greatly indebted to Peter Sheridan for all his enthusiasm, advice and first edit on the book. To my editor, Alison Walsh, for her passionate commitment and pushing me to expand. Thanks to Deirdre Nolan, Tana Eilís French, Nicki Howard and Cliona Lewis at Tivoli; Imogen Taylor and Trisha Jackson at Pan, and all at Gill & Macmillan. Also, to Clare Alexandra for her faith, and Kate Shaw at Gillon Aitken Associates. To Karen Carty at anú design.

An absolutely massive thank you to all at St Michael's House. They have a huge impact on the quality of both Saoirse's and my family's lives. To past teachers, including Ann Walker, Róisín, Jillian, Laazizi, Lucy and Louise. And present: Catherine, Clare, Dawn, Maria and Shelagh. And to Olive and Sean on the magic bus. Also, thank you to Dr Web and all at Our Lady's Hospital for Sick Children, Crumlin, and Dr Cathal Martin and the staff at Brennan's Pharmacy; their continuous care is greatly appreciated.

To Paul (who lives in Seattle, and who I miss), Tara and Thomas. And thank you to Dolores, Linda, Mary, Fran, Monica, Shelagh, and all my college pals for tolerating me so well and making insightful comments.

1

My first vision of the universe is indelibly imprinted in my head. I can still see it clearly. It had taken forever to figure out all the bits on the telescope, and I had no idea what I was looking at or for. But I never considered not knowing what I was doing to be an obstacle. I was a master of self-education and, with a stack of books beside me, I was all set.

An extra click to the right and everything became completely clear. The sky was alive and vibrating; it was so different from watching it on TV. It was exhilarating, bringing out the explorer in me. I thought of all the answers out there waiting to meet the questions in an infinite mass of possibilities. I thought of the collective consciousness. If it did exist, this was where I imagined it to live, among the stars. Masses of thoughts and ideas tangled, swarming, swimming around and through themselves in the deepest of spacescapes; concepts shaped like narrow silver fish, swimming in shoals of millions, all synchronised and making forms and bodies as they swam through space, sometimes nearing the earth. It must be at these times, when they come so near to our planet, that we have our greatest thoughts and ideas; when all of the world becomes creative and connected to itself. New ways of thinking come about, to change the world in another evolutionary way.

I got a sense of why people devote their whole lives in exchange for the chance to extract a tiny piece of its secrets, to add to the pile that will some day hopefully lead to the answer. It was endless. I went to bed to swim with the silver fish in the sea of stars.

Waking from the star sea, I fill the bath from the hot tap. The water is scalding enough to bite and turn the skin pink, a habit left over from the days of numbness. Taking my time, I put one foot in, then the other, as you do. I lower my body slowly, dip-dying it pink. Adjust to the temperature – one of life's little adjust-ments: you adjust or get out. Submerging my face, I chant in my head – *Wash away, wash away, wash away* – and whoosh up and out of the water, throwing the splashes out in a fan behind me. *Wash away, wash away, wash away, washing the dead skin away, you were once a part of me, now you are not.*

There is a certain sound to the razor dragging across the skin that warns you of a rash, like scraping a ruler along dry skin. It's all in the angle at which you hold the razor and the degree to which the blade is blunt. Shaving is one of those jobs that get you nowhere but must be constantly redone, like scrubbing soap-scum off the bathroom sink. All that energy spent removing unwanted things that keep coming back, collecting and demanding your attention, screaming to be removed.

I used to see a woman walking around my old neighbourhood who was growing out her blonde-dyed hair. She had a dark-brown cap radiating five inches in diameter from the crown of her head.

A dead-straight line ringed her head, dividing a dull chestnut-brown from honey-blonde. In an odd way I envied her, for not giving a damn. She had liberated herself. She probably had hairy armpits and legs, didn't bother with her nails. She wore no make-up, and yet, if the mood took her, she could turn around and dye her hair blonde. Or maybe she had cared before, but she was beyond it at that stage.

I wondered what she did with all those savings of minutes turning into hours into days. It must have been some fruitful activity; or she could have just cleaned more soap-scum. Maybe we need these mindless repetitive tasks, consuming much of our days, to fuzz up the focus and allow our minds to drift, dream and enter more wondrous worlds – and at other times bring us back to ground, knee-deep in reality and superfluous hair.

There is no showerhead in the bath. Standing, I fill a steel basin placed correctly in arm's reach of the bath. I empty the crisp clean water over my upturned face. It feels so clean I wish I could breathe it in, rinsing it through me as well as over me. I chant: *Wash away, wash away, wash away.*

It was after the accident that I decided to make a new life and began to wash the old one away. It wasn't really a big accident or anything, just enough to make me realise my life would be over before I began it. I had been living somebody else's life.

I lived in north County Dublin, under the disapproving glare of a mother who thought it was always best to look for the worst aspect in everything; that way you would never be disappointed. She found the worst in my best. I moved along in the clothes I thought she might like, behaving as she thought I ought to, preaching her gospel and biting my tongue. Swelling with pride, I congratulated myself on knowing the rules, at least until they changed.

I lived four doors down from her, suspended between the need to stay and the need to run away; working to pay my mortgage on time, paying it to live four doors down in a two-bedroomed white block of a semi-detached house, someone's stab at modern architecture in the seventies. I pretended to be alive and brought her shopping every week, as she didn't drive (because the other drivers on the road were far too dangerous and wild), and I called in regularly as expected. Of the five girls in my family, I was the only one who really sought her approval. Maybe that's why I never got it; maybe that's why I sought it. My two older sisters and my two younger sisters had each other; they were in pairs, leaving me at odds. So I looked to my mother.

We even pretended to be friends for a while. Pretended nothing had ever happened. In public, she might boast about her daughter, painting a picture of me I did not recognise, with qualities she thought a daughter should have. *Who is she talking about? Oh, that's me.* She even went as far as staging the odd bit of affection. 'Of course you know how talented Jean is,' she says to a neighbour, Mrs Walsh, who has known me since I was born, known my mother and my grandmother. Then, just to completely do my head in, the next time we meet Mrs Walsh she discloses, 'And you do know Jean has always had a bit of a problem with her hormone balance.' She holds her fingers pinched together to indicate how small a problem it is, and with her other hand she rubs my lower back in small circular motions, while we stand on the cracked pavement. I smile and wait for her to stop touching me.

Then the accident came out of nowhere. I met Mrs Walsh on my own. She was in the supermarket, near the entrance to the fruit and veg section, and I had just come through the checkout.

As soon as she spotted me, she noticed my bags weighing me down, on the verge of pulling my arms out of their sockets. I had decided to walk and underestimated the weight of the shopping once again. She insisted I take a lift home with her, her gappy-toothed grin shifting from side to side when she spoke, drawing attention to her prominent chin, where several long hairs had sprouted. I smiled and agreed, wondering about the sense of taking a lift from somebody whose reaction time was probably ten times the norm.

I would have asked the checkout girl to keep an eye on my shopping while I helped Mrs Walsh, but I knew from past experiences that she did not appreciate any interference with her shopping; when the wire basket got too heavy, she preferred to put it on the ground and move it along the aisle with little kicks. She must have got fed up with people asking her, 'Do you need any help?' because she got quite snappy if you did. So I just stood at the door and waited, hoping I never reached the stage where I couldn't be bothered to use tweezers on my chin.

Her chin wasn't the only thing about her that jutted out, and her shopping wasn't the only thing she got stubborn about. In a long line of houses, hers was way out of line. It had been built long before planning permission was ever seeded in a planner's head. Despite the persuasive tactics of the County Council, she couldn't be budged. They figured it wouldn't be good for public relations if they brought one of the oldest people in the community into court for eviction, so they settled on a sitting-her-out plan.

Mrs Walsh finished her shopping – she had selected three items – and we made our way to the car park. I should have known as soon as I saw the alarming shade of red. It made me take a jump-step backwards. Everyone acknowledges that red is the colour of hazards, danger and blood. Why would anyone choose a red car?

People who opt for red are often irresponsible and reckless. Insurance companies have long recognised that red cars are involved in the highest percentage of collisions by far. Big mistake: I got in.

To be fair to Mrs Walsh, we didn't have a chance. We were about to take a hairpin turn to the right when a car flew around the corner, over-shot the turn and smashed straight into us. Time slowed down and stopped; I could see the scarlet bonnet, the pause button came on, and then the black car came directly towards us. A bang cut through the slow-motion silence, slicing it in two. We were thrown forward, rag dolls restrained by seat-belts, and flung back. Then everything stopped and we stepped back into ourselves. We appeared to be fine, although the front of the car was completely mangled by this unexpected force out of nowhere.

Mrs Walsh took it all very well; I considered this could be due to the fact that she lived in a different time zone anyway. I was a bit bruised, very much shaken and still breathing.

I got home, locked the door and stopped eating. I just drank coffee, smoked cigarettes and stared for six weeks. At the end of that time, I was ready to seize control. No longer would I drift along letting life happen to me. I was going to make the life I hoped for happen, make the family I dreamt of, while I still had the chance. I would start again from the beginning.

I dropped the keys on the table and reminded the real-estate agent not to put the sign up for days. I told him my solicitor would handle everything. I could not be contacted otherwise. Six years I had lived in that house. When I first entered it, it filled me with ideas and shiny visions. It only needed a few adjustments to make everything fall into place. I moved things around and tried to figure out what it could be. Six times I painted just the kitchen.

It went from pale meadow-yellow to bluebell, terracotta, sage and a yellowy orange; finally, after colour fatigue, I painted everything white. Now I could see that painting the kitchen would never change anything. But the years of waiting had: it was now worth six times what it had been in 1994. Now it would support me, instead of me working for it.

Working my way down the ever-decreasing list of things to do, I drove to the bank, rearranged my accounts, picked up boxes – which unfortunately were oddly shaped, quite flat and very wide. I think they were lettuce boxes. They would have to do; time was running out. I got back to the house. On the way to the telephone, I kept getting distracted by piles of things calling out to be organised. *Pack this with that and put that over there. You're coming with me and you are not.* I made it to the phone and booked a moderate bed-and-breakfast on the south side. Apparently I was incredibly lucky to get anything at such short notice; I didn't know that Dublin was all the rage. In any case, the woman on the other end of the line did not want to let it go until I fully appreciated the situation, so I assured her I did.

It was time to attack the house. I became a whirling dervish, flinging things in the perfect directions, until I was left with a huge volume of rubbish, a moderate amount of things to be stored and a manageable pile of things that absolutely had to go with me or my life would never be the same.

Like my navy-blue handbag that I got for my eighth birthday. Its shiny imitation leather was coated in plastic and it had a white contrasting trim running along the edges. All my treasures were stored inside it – my Avon vanilla-ice-cream-shaped lipstick, my princess jewellery set, a pair of Barbie doll's shoes… I had kept it so close to me, it would have seemed impossible to lose it. The only explanation was that it must have slipped through a time warp. I'm looking forward to the day it drops out of the sky and lands at my feet.

As the day darkened, I closed the curtains, making sure every possible peeking-crack was covered over. I was a bit worried that my mother's instinct for zooming in on my worst disasters would kick in and she'd come snooping around. I turned the radio off and worked quietly and quickly. My heart beat in my ears as I opened the front door and started packing the bags into the car in the dark. I was making my escape. I imagined my life in danger. I could be caught and killed at any moment.

I made the final check: everything seemed to be in order. The items for storage were clearly labelled and the rubbish was stacked by the back door. I left a note for the estate agent and one for the new owners explaining the foibles of the house. As I shut the door for the last time, I could hardly contain my excitement. Inside the car, I put on the central locking. I was overcome with giddiness, heading off in the dark to live on the other side of the city. *I am going to be new and shiny.*

The directions to the new life were as follows: stay on the road with the twists and turns, minding the accident black spot, until you come to the next village. Drive straight through and, about a mile down the road, you'll see a cluster of houses. It's the third on your right, with the monkey-puzzle tree in the front; you can't miss it.

The bungalow was snuggled into a slope. Its stone walls protruded at the base, and it clung to the ground as though it might be flung off if the earth were to spin too fast. If I was going to sever my own roots, I might as well live somewhere well grounded. I parked the car in the gravel drive and crunched my way up to the house. There is great satisfaction to be had in

8

crunching gravel, and it had the added benefit of being a reliable people-detector in the quiet of night. The house was situated perfectly in relation to the neighbours – far enough away to give me my own space, yet still within screaming range, should there be a need for it. It was painted sunshine-yellow, probably to compensate for the lack of sunshine in this fragment of the world. The entrance was Dublin blue and there were terracotta pots overflowing with unidentified vegetation.

On opening the door, I was hit by the contrast between the outside of the cottage and the modern renovation inside. All the walls were white and the floors were warm cherry-wood laid down in narrow strips. Against this backdrop, everything had been carefully arranged. There was an immediate sense of order in every room, far less clutter than my old home had. In the living room stood an oversized olive sofa with hairy mammoth cushions. The fireplace was charcoal slate with gas flames – this appealed to me; heat without ash, turned on by the flick of a switch – and a cream tufted wool rug was spread out in front of it. I let my rucksack drop and went to check the rest of the place out.

This house reflects a precise mind with a good eye for space and balance. Whoever lived here before knew the importance of the empty spaces left between one thing and the next. The structure is cut in two by the hall. On the right-hand side there is the living room, and behind it a glass-and-steel kitchen, which leads out to the garden. On the left-hand side of the hall run four doors. Each of these rooms appears to be somewhat smaller than it should be. The first door opens to a small bedroom at the front of the house, the second to a bathroom, the third to a walk-in closet, and last in line is the main bedroom. Everything in this room is white except the floor and a sizable square of greenery seen through the window facing onto the rear garden.

The telephone made its presence felt at the end of the kitchen counter. I made a mental note not to have it connected. As I brought in my bags and boxes, the sun showed its face – a good sign. Getting down to organising my belongings, I found a place for everything. The house had great storage; it had secret drawers and cupboards all over, waiting to enclose items. I found one for T-shirts, corners for socks, jeans, knickers, shirts, belts, dresses and flop-around-the-house clothes. Then I went on to organise bathroom products, leisure objects and miscellaneous items. Only when all the items were away in their places did I go and make a cup of coffee and relax. It looked like I had always lived here. Maybe a different me had grown up here.

It was after I had sunk into the sofa that I detected light flooding into the room from the ceiling. There was a large pane of frosted glass, edged with beading and set into the ceiling, connecting the living room to what must have been an attic. If there was light coming from there, it meant there must be a room with a window hiding under the roof. Moving from room to room, I checked all the ceilings for an entrance, unsuccessfully. Then, positioning a chair under the window and balancing books on top, I climbed haphazardly up and pressed against the glass. It didn't budge. I ran my finger along the edges; a splinter caught me, but the glass was sealed. I thought it was odd; there must be a way up. I went outside and circled the house – and there in the back garden, I spied it, just where it should be, at the centre topmost part of the roof: a small square skylight.

Determined to find my way in, I scanned the walls and ceiling of the front bedroom. When I was satisfied there could not be an entrance, I moved on to the bathroom. Next, I opened the door to the walk-in closet, and there it was: a small door about three feet high, with a simple steel handle, set into the back wall. I was amazed I had missed it the first time.

I stepped into the closet. Warm, dusty air met me as I pulled open the miniature door. The first thing I saw was a stone wall directly in front of me, about two feet away. Poking my head in cautiously, I quickly looked both ways. There was a space two feet wide running the entire length of the left-hand side of the bungalow. Behind the main bedroom, the blackened space looked empty. The other way, behind the bathroom and front bedroom, a set of narrow stairs climbed the wall and led to the source of light.

If it had been darker, I'd never have gone up. I ducked my head and went through the narrow doorway. Up the stairs I crept, and peered over the top edge.

The whole attic could be taken in with one glance. It had a slanted ceiling and the same cherry-wood floor. There was the skylight in the centre, and below it sat a telescope, with a three-legged stool and a pile of books on the floor beside it. That was when I discovered the universe.

Out of the shower and down the meandering road to the village, flanked on both sides by wild hawthorn hedges and ditches hundreds of years old, I make my way to the shops. I notice a pale-yellow sun to one side and a low, faded moon to the other. I make myself take notice of my existence in the universe. I am walking between the sun and the moon on Planet Earth.

The hunger awoken inside me continues to grow; I want to learn more, to be more. I can make this world work for me. And in that moment a decision crashes to earth and lands in my head. I know with certainty what I'm going to do. I'm going to have a daughter. This is the place and the time for my family. I can do this. I can do anything.

I picture it as I walk along. The signs are all good. I will have to find a father, of course, but that's OK; she will still be all mine. I have enough money, hatched by my old house, to last a few years if I'm careful, and an abundance of love. We could start a new life together, and during the nine months' wait, I'll learn all about babies and the stars. Whatever I need to know, I can find. I just need a presentable man.

The shop's opening times on the door do not correspond with the door itself. They clearly read, 'Lunch time – 1:00 to 2:15', and yet it stands still, dark and locked. No mention of a holiday or a death; I can't find a reason for this. I decide to wait longer because I want to complete my mission. I saunter in the direction of the field to the side of the shop.

The field marks the end of the town. It has an old stone wall, repaired in a modern style and in ruin again; this leads up to another hawthorn hedge, which runs along the winding road leading back out of town. It is an in-between town, the kind you see passing swiftly by through a car window. There is no reason to slow down in a single-strip town with no people about and buildings that are uninteresting and old. If you caught sight of the pub, you would think that even if food were available it couldn't be fresh on account of the low turnover of produce. That would be your first thought, closely followed by a feeling of sympathy for the people born into the town. There wouldn't be time for a third because you would already be gone.

Most people seeking property in the neighbouring counties of Dublin want more than this. They are escaping not only from, but also to. And that 'to' requires features of interest, such as the shoreline, a river, hills and valleys or a pretty village more substantial than Kilreadon. It has one closed mini-supermarket, two pubs (one of which sports a petrol pump), a tiny church with a train station behind it (an occasional train is known to stop), a knick-knack shop with everything you need that the other shop hasn't got. Oh, and, most important, it has a miniature primary school. Behind its quiet face there must be lives, after all, hidden throughout the surrounding area.

The baby will have to be a girl. Having grown up in a house with my mother and four sisters, I wouldn't know what to do with a boy if you plonked one on my lap. But a girl I would know before she was born. I know her already. Loosely hugging myself, I watch my feet as I let my legs swing outwards in arches and land in front of me. I'm lost in daydreams until the most peculiar thing comes into sight. As I bend over and take a closer look, it becomes apparent it is the leg of a cat. The paw is still intact; the fur ends just below the knee, exposing the joint, like a fur sock pulled just halfway up.

I share this unexpected event with my daughter-to-be. Straightening up (I can take anything in my stride), I say out loud, 'Now if a boy found that, he'd probably pick it up and chew on it.'

'And if a girl found it, she'd probably bring it home, put a dress on it and call it Paw-Paw,' replies a deep voice from behind me.

Jumping back, I spin around to find a tall, broad man, with bear-hug arms and a grin in his eyes. Despite my fright and before I have the chance to put my guard up, I can't help but be attracted to this stranger. A manly man, with the wit to hold his own. The type of man who puts his hand up in the air and calmly catches the ball that no one saw coming.

Perhaps I'm reading too much into it, but arms like that look like comfort to me; a place in which to yield and abandon oneself, a place of passion. This is a magic land where thunderbolts strike when you think about them. Ask for a presentable man and he appears. I should have moved here years ago. I had better be careful what I think.

'Sorry, I didn't mean to frighten you,' he says, clearly amused.

'I'm sorry, I didn't realise there was anyone here.' I feel a blush creeping up my neck and a nervousness inside. This seems to amuse him further.

'Were you looking for something?'

'Yes, the shop – it doesn't seem to be open yet, for some odd reason.'

'I'm late; I'm minding it for a friend. Come on in.'

Clearing my throat, I follow him self-consciously. We enter the cool, dark shop, but I feel the air is alive between us. I can't think straight. What am I here for? Is he watching me? *Right,* I say to my head – *keep calm and just think basics, and that will have to do for now. Milk, bread, and what could I get that would reflect an interesting personality?*

'Are you passing through?' he asks, moving behind the counter.

'Passing though what?' I reply, before I have the chance to think about what I'm saying.

'Are you on holidays or just passing though the town?'

'Oh, I'm renting a place by the train tracks.' I replace the tin of tuna fish I knocked off the stack onto the floor. He pretends not to notice.

'Really? What place is that?'

'It's called Sunshine House.'

'I know it. So is it living up to its name?'

'So far, so good.' I approach the counter. 'Do you sell any beer?'

'You'll have to go to one of the pubs for that... Tell you what – that's a long way to walk carrying beer. If you like I could drop it up to you.'

14

How does he know I walked? Of course he does: there's no car outside. 'That would be great, if it isn't too much trouble.'

He leans in closer, handing me my change. Our skins briefly touch, sending a charge though me. He looks directly into my face and says, 'No trouble at all. It would be my pleasure.' I can barely stand.

Leaving the shop, I am astounded: this is the one I was destined to be with, love at first sight, the father of my child. We met over a dead cat's paw. I do have a habit of getting overexcited sometimes. I can get a crush on a man and it will completely consume me. I reach a state where I can think of nothing else. It is the one area in my life where I dive right in. It could be because I have no memories of my father, not even a photo or a description. I have no blueprint to work from, so all possibilities are still open with regards to men.

Despite the strength of my feelings if the maddening infatuation isn't returned, it can die as suddenly as it began. I reckon the time-frame in which to work something out only extends to about three weeks. This, combined with my general fear of all things living, means I have had very few actual relationships with men.

This man seemed to know the effect he was having on me; and, because I'm in the first day of the dangerous three weeks, there is little I can do but wait and see what happens. The only way out at this stage would be to pack up and jump on the next train. Alternatively, I could drive...but I want to see him.

I flutter around as the darkness falls, trying to distract myself from the mounting panic in my stomach. OK; the house is clean. I'm clean. Thank God I shaved. I put clean glasses in the freezer to chill them for the beer. My skin is damp and threatening to break out in a nervous sweat at any moment. Music – something modern, off-beat and interesting. I pick 'Godsdog' by De Phazz and play it on repeat, just loud enough for background noise.

There's a knock at the back door. Why did he do that? Did he know the previous owner? It's probably his ex-wife's house I'm renting. Taking one last look in the mirror, I open the door and realise, as I'm about to welcome him in, that I don't know his name. He offers me it before I ask, and sets a crate of green-bottled German beer on the kitchen counter. It's Liam, a name for a wild Irish man with a wild heart. I tell him my name is Jean.

I ask Liam how much I owe him for the beer. He turns, calm and self-assured, and says, 'Share one with me and we'll call it quits.' This man is comfortable with his place in the universe, not like me.

The thought of the universe is quickly followed by the thought that we each have only one life to live and this is the start of mine. Spontaneity forces its way out of me.

'Come on, grab some cushions from the living room; I want to show you something.' Capping two beers with the frosted glasses, I bring him to the passageway. We go into the closet and through the magic door. We climb the stairs, I feel Liam's eyes on me and I lead him to the stars.

As we reach the telescope, a girl-giggle escapes me. 'Look, it's the universe. Pretty cool, huh?' *Oh, God, I just said 'pretty cool'; what's happening to me?* Thousands of tiny doors open and shut inside me, chancing and dancing to let him in. Chancing that this could happen.

'Pretty cool, all right,' he smiles, but his focus is here in this space and the pull between us. He brings his face closer to mine. The world falls away and something comes out of me I never knew to be in me. My mouth falls open, no words fall out; such energy, such a wondrous force, then impact.

'So what planet are you from?' he asks later, nudging his face into mine.

'A coastal town in north County Dublin.'

'And what brought you here?'

'I was escaping my mother; she was consuming me and the only things she hadn't swallowed were my feet, so they started running in the hope that the rest would follow. What about you, where are you from?'

'I'm from right here, so I had to run somewhere else – Wales. Only I wasn't consumed, I just have little bite marks from small fish.' With that, he bites my arm. We stare at each other's face, close and unflinching. 'You know you'll probably go back,' he says.

'No, I won't,' I say decidedly.

'The mother-child bond will pull you back,' he smiles. 'Specially a girl.'

'No, we don't have one. My mother didn't even see me for three days after I was born. She had a general anaesthetic, then waited for three entire days before she saw me. And she doesn't even think this is odd. If I ask her anything about it, she just shrugs her shoulders: "I just didn't get around to it. You know in those days we didn't go in for all that bonding crap."' Putting on her voice and actions, I demonstrate for Liam and explain, 'She watches a lot of American TV and fancies herself as a typical Jewish New York momma, so she has a tendency to reflect this in her speech.'

'What do you think happened?' Liam looks like he really cares.

'I don't know.' But I know the facts surrounding my birth.

Fact 1: It was an emergency birth.

Fact 2: She did not see me for three days.

Fact 3: She once remarked, 'There is a lot more to it than you'll ever understand.' And has denied saying it since.

18

Fact 4: When I was three weeks old she left me (not my sisters) with a friend for three weeks.

Fact 5: Occasionally she lets her eyes tear over and acts as though she's about to tell me something of great importance, then backs off if I give any sign that I'm interested.

I don't say these facts to Liam because I'm not sure how much I should reveal, everything or nothing. I realise he is watching me closely. 'You can tell me,' he whispers.

'I think I had a twin – one that didn't survive the birth... I think – every time my mother looks at me she sees my dead twin's face. I keep having this dream that I'm racing on an old-fashioned bike, like the one in *The Wizard of Oz*. It's in this weird landscape that's all scraggy and dark, and there are trees – bent-over ones with no leaves – and crooked buildings on both sides of the road. And the road goes up and down really steeply, and twists and turns from side to side. Someone's trying to catch me, and I'm pedalling as hard as I can. I'm gripping onto the handlebars – they're all shaky, and the vibrations are running up my arms – and I'm racing down this road, and I have the foetus of my dead twin sister in the wire basket on the front. She's my twin; I'm not going to let anyone take her away from me. I won't let anyone catch us.'

Something changes in his face, somewhere around the mouth and the corners of his eyes. I know he knows. It is a recognition, and he will tell me, we will tell. I feel so safe.

Light streams in through the skylight, blinding me. I shade my eyes while I transcend from a sleeping state to a waking one. A warm rush spreads through me as I remember the night before. In our bed of crumpled cushions and duvet, I stretch my arms to the tips

19

of my fingers, and then my back, and then my legs with my feet arched and pointed. Turning onto my side, I push my way through the duvet to see him. He's gone.

I listen for sounds downstairs. I can't hear anything. What did I expect – to be a real person with another real person? I drove him away, I said too much, he saw too much. He understood, all right: I was either a nut or just too much to take on. I fucked it up. I spoke unchecked, unfolded, a collection of thoughts not censored. I knew I shouldn't but I couldn't stop myself. I wasn't meant to be with people. I'll probably frighten my daughter away too. I should be a monk, put a clamp on my head, stitch up my mouth, stop my head, my never-ending screaming head.

I lie still. I stay still for ages; there are no sounds. Slowly the silence fills my ears, it rolls over my face and up my nostrils, suffocating me. I focus on lifting my leaden arm, then letting it crash back down with a thud against the unyielding floor, breaking the silence.

He went back to Wales. He left a pebble by the bed. Two straight lines of limestone intersect the entire violet-grey, perfectly shaped and balanced, ordinary pebble. I don't want him if he doesn't want me. He came crashing into me out of nowhere. He wasn't even wearing red; there was no warning.

I stand at the sink with my eyes directed towards the window and replay every detail of every word and vision, searching the clips of film for any sign it was as meaningful for him as it was for me, any sign he'll come back. I run the films for a couple of weeks, until they fade. Picking up the tapes, I slide them back into their cases, shelve them in a section towards the back of my head and close the door.

2

The curtain lifts and a faint breeze drifts across the room, promising relief in this hot September morning. It lightly touches the damp, creased sheets and brushes against my skin. The light plays on the whiteness of the sheets, defining every peak, valley and groove, a study in shape and form; the variations are infinite. It is unusually hot for this time of year, and the air smells ripe with the fruits of summer's end. A crow squawks in the distance and the sound of the odd car passes by.

My breasts are swollen. I run my fingers over my smooth brown belly, curving outwards where my daughter lies. She moves in a slow rumble, rearranging herself. I press my palm firmly against her in response and try to make out her shape. The book is still open on the bed on Week 28 – the final week of the second trimester.

I glance over at the piles of books against the wall. There are three sections, each with its own thing going on: books to be read on the left, books I already read but might go back to in the middle and books I'm completely finished with on the right. Within each section, the three topics are pregnancy, astronomy and fiction. The pregnancy pile is shifting to the right most frequently.

I have developed an insatiable thirst to learn. I have wasted so much time. Devouring information and experiences, I play *Opera for Beginners* and watch *Open Science* at night. I am amazed to discover your television can pick up microwave radiation from the farthest points in outer space. All you have to do is tune in to an empty channel and look at the speckles dancing on the screen. A certain percentage of them come from microwaves far beyond our galaxy, produced by extremely violent explosions. And there they are, dancing between MTV and RTÉ 1.

Some nights I sit (with my legs apart to accommodate my ever-expanding belly) in the attic, one eye pressed to the telescope and a book at hand, trying to piece the universe together; imagining our planet going around a star, until I get dizzy.

I hover on being a well-educated person. I don't quite own words well enough to pronounce and spell them with ease, to express my ideas to others in a satisfactory way. But I understand them. I am big on concepts.

Having no syllabus, I let one thing follow another. Someone on a Psychology of Child Development programme might say something to spark an interest that I follow up. Each spark triggers the next. I leave it to chance where it will lead me. I believe in 'When the pupil is ready the teacher will appear.' I just don't believe in God when it comes to asking for help. It is important to me to make sure my daughter has a good education, both academic and in life. The first lesson will be her own value, having her needs met and feeling secure.

My daughter kicks inside me. I have slept away most of the day and a shadow is creeping across us; I hope it creeps from the past and not the future. A worm niggles in my head.

✳

22

I am thankful that the sick-as-a-dying-dog morning sickness is gone. It came and stayed for twenty-four hours a day. Lifting myself carefully, I head along the well-worn path to the freezer, where my stock of Double-Chocolate Magnums waits for me. I ignore the fact that the amount of ice-cream I am buying will be my financial ruin, with no income. Instead, I congratulate myself once again on having traded the habit of sucking on cigarettes for the one of sucking on chocolate ice-creams.

I am enjoying my newfound freedom in calorie heaven. After all, it wouldn't be wise to diet during pregnancy. I savour the chocolate layers sitting at the kitchen table. They say that when you lose weight it's from the neck down: the first loss can be seen just below the chin, and it progresses until eventually the thighs and calves are as slim as the rest of the figure. I wonder, could this be why so many women are pear-shaped? We keep starting diets that we don't follow through. I eat a peach to make sure the baby has peachy skin.

The phone looks at me. I recently had it brought to life in case I need it for the baby.

I crunch my way through the gravel. A train screeches by, sending tremors throughout the neighbourhood. If you didn't live here, you'd wonder how people could live with a noise like that. Every time I hear its piercing noise I think of the head found on the tracks, the first week I arrived. It belonged to a patient from the psychiatric hospital nearby. He had given up the struggle to be sane and thrown himself on the tracks, at the critical moment of the train's approach. The rest of his body was dragged hundreds of yards down the rails. All the secondary-school kids were sent home. The stationmaster didn't think they would be up to the journey to school, with the shock, and a boy called Sean threw up.

*

23

My neighbour Carol has an open face. I like her and her partner, Matt. They are a young, computer, casual-clothes, work-hard-play-hard sort of couple. And I found them to be friendly. In different circumstances, I could have been one of them. She is in her front garden, taking care of her large collection of conifers and heathers. I am more of a succulent and cactus person, myself; maybe I should be living in Arizona.

'When's your baby due?' She pushes back her hair with the unsoiled part of her forearm and smiles.

'Around Christmas-time.'

'You must be really excited.' She makes her way over.

'Yes, I can't wait. I already have her cot ready, and stacks of clothes and nappies.'

'Oh, do you already know that you're having a girl?'

A little embarrassed, I laugh. 'Well, I don't know from a scan or anything, but I just sort of think she'll be a girl.'

'Absolutely – people very often know whether they're having a boy or a girl. My sister has three kids and she knew with every one of them.' Carol wholeheartedly believes this, and she's making an effort to put me at my ease. She is one of those people who see the best in others.

'That's true; I've often heard of that. Well, I'd better get to the shops – I have to be home soon; I'm expecting a phone call.' I make like I'm in a rush.

'Don't forget, if you need anything, we're here – anything at the shops or whatever; you're welcome to call.'

'Thanks, thanks a lot. Well, I'll see you.'

'Bye. Take care, Jean.'

'OK…well, bye, then.' I turn and go.

It's my nature. I'm not really a people person. It isn't that I don't care; it's just that chitchat isn't my thing. I do much better

24

one-to-one when I get to know someone. It takes me a long time to get to know anyone, so by the time I'm ready, they've given up on trying to be friends.

I tried going to a counsellor once, to help me establish better relationships. I arrived at my appointed time. I sat in her garage converted to a room. I looked around; there was a heavily carved bar, complete with bottles hanging upside down and cocktail parasols in a glass. The carpet had an orange-and-brown swirling pattern. There in the middle of it sat a woman in a silver tracksuit and runners, looking like she was waiting to be contacted by aliens.

How could I talk to a woman dressed like that? I made my excuses. I changed my mind. I left and made my way to the nearest bookshop and found the Self-Help section.

I'm ready to give birth now. The novelty has worn off, and I feel I have put in sufficient effort and seriousness to reap the rewards. I'm getting restless; this adventure is turning into a three-months-too-long voyage.

Picking up the book, I scan through the information relating to the twenty-eighth week of gestation for any insights I may have missed. If she were to be born now, she would have a ninety per cent chance of survival. It would still be a struggle for her to breathe with her underdeveloped lungs. She would need assistance coping with the air we breathe. Her skin is covered in a waxy substance to prevent all thirty-seven centimetres, approximately nine hundred grams, of her becoming waterlogged in her watery world. Her eyes are open, and I can feel the rhythms of her own personal sleeping and waking patterns. I imagine her eyes slowly blinking as she turns to the light glowing through my skin.

*

The air runs about in waves. It races around the corner of the house and down the path; it's looking for leaves. What's left of the leaves is stuck in corners decaying, already in the process of becoming next year's nutrients. The brittle trees crack into the faded sky and the red bricks and terracotta pots have darkened with permanent moisture. Even the Hostas know when it's time to retreat; curling in on themselves, they sink below the clay surface like the feet of the Wicked Witch of the East.

People draw back into their homes. Only cars move about, taking them from one enclosure to the next, and I take comfort in the solid walls of my own home. Listening to the rain, I'm glad I am not a creature in the wild. It's a blustery day, as Christopher Robin would say to Winnie-the-Pooh. I rearrange Pooh Bear, along with Piglet and other friends waiting by the baby's cot. There's a rummaging noise from behind the wall, in the crawl space. It sounds like someone's moving furniture around in there. I picture a large black crow pushing a miniature red velvet sofa along a wooden floor with its beak.

Putting on my wool coat, scarf and gloves, I go over the mandatory list in my head. Windows locked, everything off (including the washing machine; on more than one occasion I have heard of a washing machine going on fire when no one was there); I have my keys, smokes – no, I don't smoke any more (*well done, Jean*) – money and credit card.

Flicking the last light off and activating the alarm, I lock the door by turning the key three times to release the deadbolt. I waddle to the car, where the first thing I do is push the central-locking button if I'm travelling beyond the boundaries of the village or if it's dark. In this case it's both. I am on a mission to see my sister in Dublin; she's always at the closing of the Christmas exhibition at the Royal Hibernian Academy of Art, and it seems like someone who knew me before should know that I'm having a baby. It's Christmas Eve and town is going to be packed, but I know exactly how to get there and I have three alternative parking places in mind.

The traffic streams out of the city, but the free flow into it more than compensates for the need to squint in the glare of white lights in my eyes. I keep thinking I'm going the wrong way. I'm taking a chance; I don't know if I'm right to make contact or not.

Doing that bastard of a thing, parallel parking, I manage to get a space a few Georgian houses down from the Academy. Pulling my scarf over my head and across my face, I walk as quickly as safety will allow in the last week of the last trimester.

People move in a rhythmic dance around the vast stone floors, in groups and couples. The long white table of waiting glasses is set for the later arrival of crowds. No sign of Norma yet. Small bursts of laughter and hushed conversations erupt and subside. A couple move on, leaving an empty space; I step in and blot out the noise of the surrounding people.

View one: at first glance, I see a drawing of an organic life form, a single-celled organism from a minute world far removed from my own. I am transfixed; it draws me in closer. There is something familiar about it. Closer still, I realise it's not what it seems at first: it's a city. Taking a quick look at the next picture, I see it's another city. They're all pencilled cities in fine detail. This visual shift transforms one idea of a living organism to another. In front of my eyes are living and evolving cities growing on the Earth's surface. They change and develop, radiating outwards.

I am a part of this, breathing into it, coursing through its veins. Exchanging energy, parts of it die and are replaced. We each find ourselves in different places and in different roles. It grows and decays. Moving in the flow of the gallery, I am a cell in the city and I am a city of cells – millions of cells, each with its own instructions and aims. They are drawn together for whatever reason they don't know. They perform a function; they just do it. Maybe cells spend time wondering why they and their fellow cells behave as they do, why cells die, age and disappear, whether they will be remembered. Some cells seem to be exceptionally different, good or bad. Some mutate and bring us forward, others become destructive, with no distinguishing marks to set them apart from the rest.

From afar, the earth looks like a blue organism floating in a black sea, hardly distinguishable from a single-celled organism. There are layers of life starting in particles so small they are not perceptible to the human eye. They are so tiny we must peer into increasingly powerful microscopes to see them and their vast landscapes.

There are so many places of remarkable beauty in worlds parallel to our own. I am exactly where I am meant to be, in a world within a world, with endless worlds within me.

'Jean? Oh, my God, I don't believe it's you. Holy shit – what's this?' Norma shrieks, pointing at my belly. 'You're pregnant?'

'Yeah, it's me,' I laugh, 'and yeah, I'm pregnant.'

'How the hell did that happen? Where have you been? Is this why you left? Are you with the father?'

'No, this happened after and on purpose, and I'm not with the father,' I answer, enjoying every minute of it.

Norma's face shifts into seriousness. 'What did you leave for?'

'I guess I just had enough, wanted to start over again.' I hope she will get it.

'And could you not have done that without disappearing?' Anger breaks into her voice. 'Jesus Christ, Jean!'

'No, I couldn't.' I give a half-shrug; I am ready to walk away.

Norma exhales her anger and softens. 'Well, I suppose we weren't that surprised. At least, I wasn't. In a way, I was surprised you hadn't done it years ago.' We say nothing for a moment; then she suddenly points at my belly and says, 'But this certainly is a surprise, a great big one. I can't believe you're pregnant – it's so funny to see you like this. What's the story?'

'Well, I decided it was time to have a baby, so I'm having it. The father doesn't know, so it'll just be Baby and me.' I can't conceal my excitement; I'm rubbing my belly as if it's the best thing ever. Until I look up and see her judgmental face.

'So, what – you just got pregnant and you're not going to tell him?' Norma says in a tone between astonishment and disapproval. I say nothing. She changes the subject.

'Where are you living?'

'On the south side.' It is enough of an address for both of us.

'Come on, let's sit down,' she says, moving to a small cluster of tables.

'How is everybody?' I can't help asking.

'Oh...I haven't seen any of them for months. Everyone's fine. I'm sure. Wondering where you are. Or not.' She flickers her focus back and forth between me and the surface of the table. 'We knew you were OK because you sold the house and all. So we knew you hadn't been kidnapped or anything.' Norma suddenly laughs openly. 'All hell broke loose when you first left. Everyone was bitching about everything – it was unbelievable; every time we got together, there was just constant bitching. But it settled down eventually. Now, if we're ever in Mammy's, no one would dare mention your name 'cause they know it'll erupt again.' She laughs, then shrugs. 'But, sure, we hardly ever see each other anyway. Lisa was very upset; she feels sorry for you. But she's a dickhead – it's not like she ever tried to find you or anything. And

of course Mammy uses it as another one of her woe-is-me things.'
Norma leans forward in a reassuring way. 'I wouldn't blame you;
you're better off out – really, Jean, you're better off.'

We don't speak for a few minutes. Then Norma says, 'Look,
everyone has something – all families are screwed up; you just have
to get on with it. You're too sensitive; you have to detach yourself and
deal with your relationships on your own terms, set your boundaries. Ya see, if she starts with me I just say, "If you're going to start
acting like that and criticising me, I'm going," and she stops.'

'It's different for you; she likes you,' I say.

'It doesn't make any difference if she starts the Mammy thing;
you say to hell with her. You don't have to run away.'

'You don't understand: I can't say anything to her. I can't say
the things you say, and I can't pretend that it's OK, because it's
not OK. Too much happened.'

'Well, I'd rather pretend than run away. You should just get on
with it like everybody else.'

She is angry again. The strategies we employ for coping with
the monsters under the bed are too far away from each other. We
were blown outwards from a central figure. Norma and I are
about 170 degrees apart, which is closer than I am to any of my
other siblings, yet still on opposite sides of the moon.

Norma begins shifting long thin parcels of sugar on the table
randomly apart and back and forth with increasing speed. Her
face is distorting; I can't tell if she's going to cry or explode. I
don't know what to say. Then she jolts the chair back suddenly.
'Look, I have to go, call me when you have the baby.'

It wasn't good for any of us. She simply ran in a different way.
My throat constricts.

'I mean that: call me.' She turns back. 'Are you all right for
everything? Do you have people out there, friends and stuff, if

you need help or anything?' I can see the two-way pull of wanting to help and wanting to flee. If my mother sees my dead sister in my face, Norma sees everything she wants to forget. She waits for the answer she needs.

'Oh, yeah, sure. I've made some really good friends, I have everything – all set.' I keep my baby-belly under the table. I won't call her; it's easier to live separate lives, to forget, when there are no reminders. Norma and I are on different sides; all my siblings dispersed, held in different places by the greatest force, which is my mother.

A warm gush signals the time has come. At first, I think I've wet the bed. But when I stand, more water gushes to the floor. It's totally unlike peeing; it isn't a stream and there is no muscle control involved, it just falls downwards by gravity alone. The baby has stopped moving; she is still. I crouch down, rub my finger in the liquid and bring it to my nose. It has no smell.

Setting my thinking in order, I remember the action plan. Rule 1: if your waters break, go directly to hospital. Even if labour hasn't started, you will be vulnerable to infection. Rule 2: ring Carol and Matt. It's five-thirty in the morning. After much persuasion, I agreed to call when the time came; and here it is.

I make the call; the phone rings and rings and rings, no answer. I get dressed, leaving puddles of amniotic fluid all over the house. Twice I underestimate the amount there is and twice I have to change my trousers. How much can there be? I ring again; it rings and rings, and Matt answers. His voice is croaky.

I am clear and precise. 'This is Jean next door. I'm sorry to wake you, but my labour has started. Would you be able to bring me to the hospital now?'

31

There is a pause at the other end of the line.

'It would be great if you could drive me,' I say, trying to express the urgency in a subtle way.

'What are you talking about?'

Paying particular attention to my enunciation, I say, 'It's Jean. The baby's coming. I'm having the baby.'

'Oh, right – right. I'll be right over.'

Ten minutes later, I'm first gripped by excitement as I feel something happening, and then taken over by the pain. I'm ready to go, standing by the front door with my bags at my feet. Matt pulls up the drive. The pain starts in my lower back, spreading outwards in both directions until it meets at the front of my rock-hard abdomen.

Matt hops out of the car with a startled look on his face; he's poised for action.

'Right, we'd better get going.' He picks up my hospital bag. 'Have you got everything?'

I notice he looks bleary-eyed and dazed. I hope he is safe to drive. At least his car isn't red. Another wave of pain takes hold. It feels like sheets of hot metal surrounding the middle of my body, an inch under my skin. The sheets grip me in a firm vice, compressing my entire torso, while my arms, head and legs go weak with nausea. Matt doesn't know what to say. I think he's praying that I'll hold on till we get to someone who has a better idea of what to do.

We arrive at the Rotunda at five past seven. Somehow I make it through the entrance. They keep asking me stupid questions like, 'What's your last name?' It becomes apparent that I have to wait for a wheelchair to collect me. I'm about to give birth in the foyer because hospital policy says I must be collected in a wheelchair.

Two nurses arrive with the chair, and I part company with Matt. Nothing to worry about; I am in good hands.

We go down endless corridors, up in a lift (I'm momentarily distracted from the pain when they push me into the lift and leave me facing the wall), down more corridors, and the whole time they talk to me and ask questions, as though I could answer, as though I could care what they're saying. They settle me into my room, proud of their new extension. It is straight out of a hospital in TV-land.

I'm somewhere high above the ceiling. I'm falling backwards into space, floating in the black sea. There are people rushing about below me; why am I floating above them? I hear noise in the distance, a scream. I see a woman. She is throwing her head back and screaming. It sounds like me, and I watch this other self.

With a jolt, I shift back inside myself at the moment of the most unbearable pain. I am split in two like an atom as she is born at seven-twenty a.m.

The moment I look at her, I know her. We are left alone, bundled up face to face. Her eyes open wide; they have tiny white stars circling the rims of her solemn blue irises. The outer edges tilt up towards her temples; they are perfectly overarched by her brows. Her small mouth has a faint trace of a smile. She looks like a Tibetan Buddha. She is the most beautiful creature I have ever seen. The bond is so strong, we merge into each other. I cannot tell where I finish and she begins. I can't believe she is finally here. My daughter, at last. It's such a relief. I have waited so long, all my life.

✳

The nurse enters briskly, as nurses do. 'Right, now, Miss Daly, we'll have to take Baby along for her tests.' She approaches to remove my daughter from my arms.

'What for?' I pull my baby in closer to me, raising my chin.

'Standard tests.' She looks at me impatiently, then proceeds to check her uniform for creases while she waits for my reply. This is the same nurse who told me I would not be giving birth till the end of the day, only a moment before I split in two.

She shifts her feet to a firmer stance. 'It's for Baby's good. Now you wouldn't want to put Baby's health at risk, would you?' She looks triumphant, assuming her attack has been successful.

'I want to go with her,' I declare.

'Doctor wouldn't have that,' she says.

'She's my baby, and she's not going without me.' Doctors may be gods in Nursie's world, but not in mine. I square my shoulders, sending animal warfare signals. I want to make sure she is absolutely clear about where I stand on this issue; I am prepared to fight.

'Right, then, I'll go and see what Doctor has to say.' And off she goes.

She marches back ten minutes later with another nurse and a wheelchair. 'Now, if you would like to get into the wheelchair, Nurse Kinnaghan will carry Baby and we'll bring you along to Doctor's clinic for Baby's tests.'

I relax. I'm going with her, to watch over her. They won't be doing any experiments on my baby. No pricking her with a pin while they count how many seconds it takes for her blood to clot or her tears to stop. There will be no student doctor trying for the first time to insert a needle in her tiny, hard-to-find veins – not with me there to protect her. No one is going to touch a thread of gold on her fine fluffy head.

Having successfully braved the standard tests, we settle down together to feed. I lift my nightshirt and take my engorged breast from my feeding bra. Holding my little daughter's head, I position her open bird-mouth to my nipple and help her latch on. She sucks firmly, biting with her little gums. Several jets of milk squirt to the back of her throat, and she swallows by reflex. Her suck is strong, easing the pressure on my breast as the milk is released.

The first flow is thick and creamy, full of fat. In a few days the thinner milk, tinted with a vague hue of blue, will follow. A few minutes on one breast, then the other. Her face is sticky, her mouth grows slack; exhausted, she falls back into sleep. The milk runs between our skins in a warm damp patch.

She is everything I thought she'd be and much more. My love for her is overwhelming. I can bite it. If I move away from her it seeps from me and permeates the atmosphere, seeking her. It cannot help but find her and wrap itself about her.

I wonder where her father is, for the first time in a long time. Would he love her? How could he not? How could he not know he has a child in this world? Will he not feel it in his wild heart? Will he look to the sky and catch a fleeting glimpse of his daughter, the way I sometimes see my twin? Will he feel this missing piece that he can never pin down, like an excited particle that moves away every time you near it?

He isn't in the plan. The plan is for my daughter and me to live happily ever after. It isn't complicated. I will make her happy. I have acquired enough knowledge to nurture a happy, well-developed, well-adjusted, balanced child. In this task, the significance of remembering what it feels like to be a child cannot be overstated.

*

My mother stood before me, staring down on me. I was in my underwear, my hair dirty and tangled from play. Shame and disquiet trembled through me as she passed judgments down. My bare arms and legs twisted, looking for something to grasp, vines seeking support, but the air was empty and they found only themselves to cling to. I dug my toes into the bare soil, rooting myself. My feet in the earth and the clouds moving overhead. I stood and waited for all to pass, as I knew it would. That was the one thing I could count on: this too would pass, there was an end to everything.

If you know how to handle yourself, most things are endurable. Pulled about by the hair, the main thing to remember is to go with the flow. With a little shift of the mind, the shouting and the screaming move off into the distance. Pain is only pain, just follow where your hair takes you. Look how all the angles of the rooms change. You can see the front room sideways, follow along into the sideways kitchen. Wherever you're led, just follow, making sure to keep your feet moving fast enough. Up the stairs. To your room. It all passes.

'You must miss your mother at a time like this. I'm sure she's looking down on you. Is there anyone you'd like to get in touch with?' asks Nurse Kinnaghan.

I told her I live on my own – my mother passed away, friends emigrated, I moved a few times, lost touch; but that's OK, because life is about change. I have some new friends; she's seen Carol and Matt visit, and I am vague about other people. I am normal, it's just circumstances.

I notice a lot of whispering before anyone reaches my bed. I figure it's either because our happiness has a tranquil effect on others, or because word has got out that I am difficult and not to be messed with. My daughter lies sleeping soundly in the bassinet, swaddled in a pea-green blanket, a sugar pea still in the pod. The other mothers are busy trying to feed babies that won't eat, calling nurses and ducking projectile vomit. My daughter is different; she is quiet and calm. She doesn't turn beetroot and scream. Only once did she let out a cry to be fed; at that, it was really too soft to be a cry. She stares into my eyes, suckles and drifts back into sleep. Ours is a peaceful, orderly corner of the ward.

After Nurse Kinnaghan calls a taxi for us, she brings us down to the nurses' station. We sign a form to say how very thorough and efficient they were and how we would never consider holding them responsible for anything bad now or in the future.

'Have you decided on a name for her yet?' asks Nurse Kinnaghan.

'Sugar Pea.'

'Oh.' She thinks this incredible, is about to protest the very idea of it, when she realises it was a joke, and starts to laugh. Then, looking back at my face, she realises it wasn't, and decides the best thing to do is just carry on with the procedure.

The thing is, I just can't find the right name. I want it to be perfect. I want it to fit her – but how do you name a Tibetan-Buddha baby who may grow up into a thirty-five-year-old mathematician or a sixty-four-year-old artist living on a self-sufficient homestead? I'll wait. The perfect name will come.

'And what last name are you giving her?'

'My own – Daly.'

'Are you Jean Daly, and is Sugar Pea Daly your child?'

'Yes and yes.'

'And is this child in front of me Sugar Pea Daly?'

'Yes.'

She checks the name on the bracelet tagged to Sugar Pea's arm. She reads aloud the name and number on it, ticking it off the list. She hands it to me. Then she unsnaps the fasteners along the legs of Sugar Pea's baby-gro, unsnaps the bottom of her vest and lifts the two together to reveal a white sticker, with my name, address and hospital number, plastered to her back. This sticker came into use the year two sets of babies were switched and one went missing, later to be found in the pram of a woman still in a state of acute grief for the child she had lost.

Nurse Kinnaghan escorts us through the corridors, down in the lift and out the main entrance. She wishes us well as she hands Sugar Pea to me in the back of the taxi.

Nearing home after the endless journey, I finger the name bracelet in my pocket. I will put it away and make it special. Some things are innately special, and others you make special because of their associations or something you invest in them. This name-tag is special. I will save everything for Sugar Pea, every piece of her puzzle. I will find her a name that encompasses all possible choices of being. When she grows up, she will be exactly who she wants to be.

3

We move to our own beat and let rhythms establish themselves. Feeding in silence with Sugar Pea nestled in my arms, I search her face for a name and play with her toes. There are freesias on the table in the kitchen, and stacks of freshly laundered baby clothes. Sugar Pea thrives on affection, her cheeks grow fat on it.

When we get home, Carol is the first to greet us. She takes great delight in having an excuse to ooh and ah over the baby garments. She takes even greater delight in giving them to us, clothes for Sugar Pea and a mass of orange lilies in deep-green foliage for me. Holding Sugar Pea, she marvels at her features and talks about the babies she will have someday, when the time is right. In the meantime, she cuddles Sugar Pea until she knows she has to let go. Then she offers, at least three times, to babysit, it would be no bother at all. But I want Sugar Pea close to me, so close it would be impossible to lose her.

The doorbell goes into a state of shock when it rings again; this time it's Marion, with two of her children and one dog in tow. She lives across the road and has dozens of blond-headed children and an assortment of animals. At all hours of the day or night, noises can be heard coming from their direction. She holds her arms in close to herself, like a gerbil, and carries a gift wrapped in paper with naked babies sitting on clouds. I can't help but look anxiously at the dog.

As Marion passes through the doorway with the children, she says something about staying a moment, but my attention is fixed on the dog. A ridge of hair stands up on his back and his nostrils are flared as he sniffs the entrance. I bare my teeth at him, backing it up with a growl perceptible to a dog but not to the ear of the human species. I think it's best I do this, because I have a feeling he considers himself in a better position in the pecking order than his mistress and would pay no heed to the feeble commands of Marion. I shut the door firmly in his face.

I turn my attention to the children, making sure none of their fingers finds itself poking Sugar Pea in the eye. Little blond heads together, hands dangling by their sides, they stare at Sugar Pea expressionlessly. Marion peers up at me from behind her clasped hands. She always speaks so quietly that it sometimes makes me want to shout, 'WHAT? WHAT DID YOU SAY?' And her colouring reminds me of my mother. I can't be comfortable in her company. It's hard enough to live with my legs, which have taken on the appearance of my mother's and make me fear that the likeness will one day spread up me and I will become her.

'She's lovely, Jean. Look how tiny her hands are. You forget how small they are. Is she good?'

'Yes, she's great.'

'Does she feed well?'

'Yes, great, not a problem.'

'Does she get up much during the night?'

'No, not really; just the once during the night.'

'How much did she weigh?'

'Seven pounds, one ounce.'

I beam at Sugar Pea. She is incredibly beautiful. Opening the present, I can see that the dress in baby-pink is not something I'd put on her. In fact, it would make her look like she belonged to another mother, not me. I say it's lovely with what I judge to be the right amount of enthusiasm, and, after a respectable allotment of time, coffee and politeness, they go on their way.

Not a minute too soon, according to my breasts, which tingle with every thought or mention of Sugar Pea and are now achingly begging for relief. I settle on the sofa with Sugar Pea. She latches her open mouth to my breast and it surges milk, making her cough and splutter as she takes it down hungrily. My other breast starts to spurt milk of its own accord. They gush between us, on us and into Sugar Pea until the pressure subsides, leaving us saturated. I love that I can produce milk in such abundance for my baby, and I marvel at my body's ability to figure this out and do it so well. Squeezing my nipple myself, I can take aim and shoot a jet or two up to ten feet across the room. Before this, I didn't even realise there were several outlets in each nipple and that, with good pressure, it is like turning on a shower. Some day I'll have another baby and, when Sugar Pea isn't expecting it, I'll shoot her with a jet of milk as she passes.

Buzzz, buzzz, the doorbell shrills through the air. *Buzzz, buzzz...* I'll ignore it and they'll go away. *Buzzz, buzzz...* Then the rapping on the glass panel of the door starts. Irritated, I move Sugar Pea into a position where she won't fall off the sofa. Adjusting myself, I pull my top down and grab a towel for milk leakage on the way to the door.

I recognise the blurred image trying to spy through the door. Betty, Betty the bat. She started coming round four or five months ago, whenever it was she spotted I was pregnant without a wedding ring. She belongs to a Christian group so extreme they think the present Pope is too liberal and needs to tighten his rein on the flock. In the meantime, they think it's their duty to see that we don't all burn in hell. So Betty took me on as her personal project and insisted on handing me the newsletter herself, just in case a demon lurked in my letterbox and got to it first. This was despite the fact that I repeatedly told her I do not want it, I have my own beliefs, I am a practising atheist, Jew, Buddhist… Nothing would deter her.

She also has an unfortunate need to jump out in front of cars in an effort to stop them. If she succeeds, she edges her way around the bonnet, and before you can decide what to do, she's in the passenger seat, praying fervently for your soul. I learnt my lesson; now, as soon as I see her, I always hit the central locking and slowly drive around her, reasoning to myself that not only do I not need someone praying on my head as I am driving, but that the small bit of exercise she gets walking down the road and jumping out in front of cars is probably the only thing keeping her alive.

I open the door to her nodding head, flame-red lipstick and eyebrows shaved off and re-drawn higher up her forehead, making her look permanently surprised. 'Hi, Betty.' She keeps smiling and nodding and poking her rolled-up Christian revival newsletter at me. I take it and thank her, convinced that one day I will have to scrape a flat Betty off the road.

All these new contacts from the birth of a child. I have become part of the buggy brigade, up and down to the shops. Now that I have a baby, people who never tended to say hello before do so, as though I have changed in some way, have some added value that I didn't possess before. All the same, I am impressed by the general friendliness and good will (sometimes misplaced, such as with batty Betty) of the community. I think this must be the way people act. I find a certain security in believing I have some sort of place in the community. I think they're nice enough, but I want to keep my space.

Sugar Pea manages to snuggle in closer to my thigh where she lies on the sofa beside me. It amazes me, as she has no visible means of propelling herself forward or from side to side. It must be a type of homing instinct in action. If I move up the sofa a bit, within an hour she'll be there, smack up against me. You would have to film it and play it back in slow motion to reveal how she does it. I lean over to smell her; she smells like herself. I pick up her fist, open it by pushing my nose under her warm clenched fingers, and then move her opened hand down my face. I kiss the crease that runs across her palm. Her eyes watch me, waiting for my next move. Out of the corner of my eye, I catch a fleeting glimpse of something running low along the skirting of the far wall, about the size of a cat. I turn quickly, but it's gone.

Continuing my education, I decide it's a good time to learn about numbers. It could come in very handy, taking into consideration that more than one mathematician reckons they can explain all of life in a formula. Of course, this doesn't take into account the theory of chaos, which, despite all the advancement it has led to, indicates we can never find the formula because by the time you worked out all the possible outcomes for a given event in a given moment they'd have changed. The universe is in a constant state of creativity, and the rules can change at any moment. Einstein tried to prove it wrong. He couldn't live in a world where the answer was that there was none, and neither could I.

If you lined up a million atoms back to back (not taking into account that there are always gaps or that they have no backs), they would only measure half the width of the average zero typed on a standard page. Within one of those atoms, the nucleus is so small that its solid matter would amount to just one millionth of a billionth of an atom; the rest of the atom is empty. So, because we are made up of atoms, if we were reduced to matter alone we would be one millionth of a billionth of the size we are now; the rest is empty. This can all be worked out mathematically, if you have the time and equipment to do it...and the inclination. I'm keeping my eye open in software outlets, where I hope to come across a programme with the unique ability to download maths directly into the head via the ear.

The first layer of air is warm as a summer's day, but the breeze quickly blows this away to expose the underlying crispness that tells you it's really spring – and, at the same time, reminds you that summer is on the way. Summer is the time I long for. Winter has its compensations, such as Christmas, autumn has the leaves, and spring...despite the new life everywhere, the best part of it is knowing that summer will soon be here. The birch tree shimmers in the light and the grass is vibrant with new growth, tall and fine. I crave the heat of an average star.

The pain I feel for others is in direct, sharp proportion to my overwhelming love for Sugar Pea. I find myself opened to a vulnerability I didn't know before. I find myself not only fearing for my child but also suffering with all the children of the world. Each one is a child like mine. A little girl is found dying, made to live in a cage in a basement. Somewhere else are deaths by starvation, paedophile rings, children cast into lives of slavery, hopelessness and wars and all that they entail. The unimaginable imagined.

What pain it is to bring a child into this world. How will I protect her? I shouldn't have done it, it was the worst thing I could have done. Now I will know pain like I never knew before. There is no disconnection from your child, no detachments; no turning off the news, switching the channel, pretending you didn't see it because if you did you could no longer function in this world. I find Sugar Pea and hold her and she comforts me. *We will be all right, Sugar Pea.*

The influx of people spearing their way through our thick bubble-skin continues with the arrival of the local health nurse.

She fits into her persona comfortably, giving encouragement and offering advice in a friendly manner. She even has a trace of scattiness to put you at your ease. From her store of weight charts, food pyramids and other relevant information she provides remedies for cradle cap and dry skin, and the optimum sleeping position for Baby. She measures, weighs and records. Babies are her job. It seems to be a requirement to address the mother and child as though their first names were Mother and Baby. I retaliate by naming her Nurse.

Apparently, Sugar Pea and I were nearly lost in the system; we should have had a visit four months ago, when we first arrived home. I suspect this is due to my inability to find her an official name causing her birth records to go off course. I've read so many books of names that they are spinning in my head and appearing in my dreams.

Nurse and I sit on the sofa with Sugar Pea in the middle. I'm ready to be questioned about my mothering techniques. Nurse has on the big smile she has prepared for Baby. Just before she settles into position, it disappears and is replaced by a faintly perplexed look, which she quickly shakes off to return to her original smile.

'What is it?' I ask her.

'What do you mean?' she replies.

'You had a funny look on your face.'

'No, not at all – I was just admiring her. She looks beautiful. Her little outfit is lovely, and you obviously are doing a great job with her. Do you have good support in place?'

I give her the answer I suspect she'd like to hear, but she hasn't really shaken that look off her face and I know there's something wrong, something I hadn't pinned down before. 'She doesn't laugh,' I blurt out. 'I mean, she looks happy – and she is happy, I know she is – but she doesn't laugh. That's very unusual, isn't it? I've searched through all the books and there's no mention of babies not laughing.'

Nurse's face grows concerned. This frightens me more. *Don't look at me like that.* 'Well,' she begins, 'most babies would be laughing by now, but it doesn't necessarily mean there is anything wrong. All babies are different. It could be her personality, or sometimes a baby might be very advanced in one area and a bit slower in others. It would all balance –'

'She doesn't cry either,' I interrupt with sudden desperation.

'Really? She doesn't cry?' Nurse is taken aback; this is not an everyday occurrence.

'No.' *But can't you see it's only because she is a special girl unlike any other?* I shriek inside.

'What do you mean by not crying – do you mean she doesn't cry a lot, or hardly ever?'

'At all.'

'She doesn't cry at all?'

'No.'

'And is she well otherwise?' Nurse asks, clearly feeling her way through unknown lands.

'Well, yes, she seems fine – I mean, she eats well and sleeps and she's content.' I become aware of something eating in my side, taking sharp little bites. 'There's another thing... I know it might sound odd, but sometimes she looks as though she thinks she's falling.'

With this additional information, Nurse realises this is beyond her field of knowledge. Gathering and shuffling her charts, she mentally shifts the responsibility of finding the answers to the next level of expertise in the medical arena. Nurse will be on to Doctor, to tell Doctor all about Baby. Nothing to worry about, we'll have Baby sorted out in no time. I see her stretching her hand out to me; it lands on my wrist, which she grasps firmly and gives a little shake with every word.

'Don't blame yourself, it's not your fault.'

This is not what I want to hear; we have stepped over a line into a place where I don't want to be. I look at her hand gripping my wrist until she lets go.

Having dealt with this sufficiently in her mind, she relaxes back into normality. 'And how are Baby's bowel movements?'

Blowing away our worries, we walk briskly after Nurse has left. The gravel feels the same beneath my feet as it did yesterday, the hawthorn hedges are the same, everything is the same, except it all seems to have taken on a difference that I can't quite put my finger on. There's an ominous charge in the air. I pick up the pace so we will reach our destination and return before the sky opens

47

up. As we round a bend, a large black-and-white cow standing in the middle of the road confronts me. I'm afraid to be near a cow; they seem stupid enough to walk over you, trampling you to death without even meaning to. I'm afraid of cows and I'm afraid of dogs.

I mustn't show my fears to Sugar Pea. I mustn't pass them on to her. I turn around and head straight back to the house, straight up the road, straight up to the door. I push Sugar Pea and her buggy inside and close and lock the door. How can I protect her when I can't even find a name for her, when I am stopped in my tracks by a cow?

I must stop visualising my fears or I will make them come true.

I strip down Sugar Pea and let her have a naked kick before putting on a new nappy. She stretches out, her tummy against the fluffy blanket. She lifts her head up, bracing herself on her chubby arms. Her little bum is round and bouncy; you can't help but give it playful taps. She cannot laugh but her face is full of laughter, her eyes bright. She loves to play, and her skinny little legs give frog-like kicks. She delights in lifting her head and kicking, feeling how great she is swimming in the air. She tells me not to worry – see how much fun it is to move your arms and legs about?

Pulling Sugar Pea to me, I put her nappy on. We snuggle tightly together, sharing skinship, lost in the middle of the soft white mountains of pillow and duvet, breathing in each other's breaths, back and forth, first her, then me, until we fall asleep.

Something wakes me. It's dark outside. I hear crunching on the gravel. Lifting my head out of the covers, I freeze and strain my ears. It stops. After what I judge to be longer than the cruncher would wait, I haven't heard anything, and I reassure myself. The alarm is on, should anyone try to enter. This is not New York, where a woman could be stabbed in the street while the entire neighbourhood of witnesses stood by. This is Wicklow; my neighbours would come to my aid, just as I would to theirs, without question.

That night I dream that I wake in the night to blackness. I can't see anything, just black space. Sugar Pea is choking beside me. I know if I can only get to the light switch, I'll be able to see what it is she's choking on and dislodge it. I have to act right away. But I am paralysed. If I can just get to the light switch, she won't die. After struggling with all my strength for an endless time, I break through with a scream, waking myself drenched in sweat with Sugar Pea sleeping soundly beside me.

I don't want to go back to that dream. Making sure everything is in its place and as it should be, I kiss Sugar Pea and head for the telescope.

It's a clear night. To focus myself on the size of the universe, I always start off with the sun, reminding myself that we are orbiting an ordinary star. Its magnitude is about average, it couldn't be classified as large or small, it's middling and it's in the middle of its lifespan. It's just one of over a hundred million stars in our galaxy, and our galaxy is just one of millions of galaxies in the universe. I place myself sitting on the moon, choosing it for its solid, relatively flat surface with little to obstruct my view.

I look for black holes – not for the holes themselves, because they radiate no visible light, but for signs indicating that they are here among us. They are tracked by the effect they have on everything around them. They leave a path of destruction as they tear apart and devour anything they come across. Just once, a black hole was seen – not as itself, or by what it left behind, but as an interruption of light, as it eclipsed a star in the outer reaches of the galaxy. It was seen just once, after a lifetime of searching.

A new day, full of possibilities. Sugar Pea is just a quiet child because she is an old soul, with wisdom far beyond the range normally to be expected at four and a half months. She has a special aura about her, a knowingness. Naturally, I will follow it up and see what the medical opinion is. It's the responsible thing to do. But Sugar Pea is special; she will do her own thing in her own time. Nothing is clearly defined, nothing is definite. Something is only true until something else comes along to prove it isn't. Once we thought blue and red made purple. In reality, the purple is less than the whole of the blue and the whole of the red; the purple is what is left after all the rest of the light has been absorbed.

Having sorted the unease I was feeling, we go about our day. She's just different, and that OK; it's OK to be different.

In the evening, we decide to have our dessert – a lemon sorbet for me, and a mini lemon sorbet for Sugar Pea – in the living room. Sugar Pea sits on my lap crossways; my hand comes up her back, supporting her heavy head on her fragile, wobbly neck. Her muscle tone and strength seem to vary lately; now they're not so good. With my other hand, I spoon the last of the sorbet into her baby-bird mouth.

Just as I finish, a blue tint seeps into her skin. It bleeds through her from her mouth, radiating outwards. Her face darkens. Sugar Pea jumps in my arms, violently, lifting her whole body upwards as the spoon goes flying across the room. I tighten my grip to stop her from throwing herself up in the air. Her feet dig into the sofa and her whole body becomes rigid, causing her to rise to a half-standing position on her anchored feet. I hold on as she gasps for air with a violent sucking sound and expels it through clenched teeth. Her flesh turns from blue to purple to black. *Oh, God, don't let this be happening – she's going to die – please, no, not now. Don't take my baby away from me, not now.*

I run to the phone, with her gasping and jumping in my arms. 999...nothing. *OK, fine; just do it again – 999...* The phone doesn't work. *Fuck the phone.* I take the receiver and smash it on the phone. *Fuck you, fuck you, you stupid fucking phone.* I run with Sugar Pea straight out the front door, my bare feet running through the stones as the light is leaving the day. Straight to Carol's door, banging, they'll help us. Banging on the door – 'Carol, Matt, help me! Don't worry, Sugar Pea, you'll be OK.' She's not jumping. She's black and blue. She's limp. *Oh, God.* My stomach drops, my blood drains downwards, everything is moving downwards. Carol and Matt come to the door, pulling us in. The words propel out of my mouth so fast they tumble over one another, jumbling up. They can't understand me.

'Sugar Pea, come back, come back.' Through all the confusion, she enters back; there is life in her eyes again. I can see her. The blueness is fading.

Carol sits us down on the sofa, me still clutching Sugar Pea. She kneels beside us, frantically rubbing Sugar Pea's arms and legs, while Matt rings the ambulance. It's over, but the effects linger. Sugar Pea blinks at me. I want to retreat to our bed and never come out again, but we must wait.

A short time later, with Sugar Pea still attached to me, we rock from side to side, sitting sideways in the ambulance. The attendant asks me questions. I can see he has no idea what I'm talking about, looking at the calm child in my arms. I try to explain.

'Her arms were so black it looked as though she had elastic bands on them – you know when you were a kid and used elastics to cut off your circulation and watch your finger turn black like a dead man's finger? That's how black she turned.' It didn't register with him, he didn't understand. If she still needed help he could not help us.

'Do you think she may have been a bit cold, love?'

In the waiting room I surrender to the shock, letting it wash over me. I become unfocused, my eyes moving slowly from one point to the next, taking in all the different parts and gradually building a picture. The doctors find nothing wrong. They don't seem fazed by their inability to explain what happened to her.

'About these other things – the not-smiling stuff,' one doctor says. This one takes his casual bedside manner very seriously. 'You will be following that up with your doctor, won't you?'

'Yes. Why? Are they related? What do you mean?'

He shrugs in a noncommittal way. 'Ah, nothing. Maybe, maybe not. Not to worry.' Seeing my fear, he raises his arm to say how foolish he was even to mention it. 'No, no, really, there's nothing to worry about.'

I don't reply. I go home. The house looks like an ordinary house. I check every baby and health reference book in the house. Toxoplasmosis leaps out of one book – a neurological disease spread through cat faeces. That's it: there is a cat here. *Whatever it is, we'll fix it, I promise, Sugar Pea.*

4

The appointment for the hospital sits on the doormat with the rest of the post. Why would they make an appointment for Sugar Pea to see the top consultant paediatrician in the country? Even I have heard of Dr Baculum. I look for clues on the card. The appointment is in six weeks' time. They don't appear to be too concerned about Sugar Pea. We are to be at the Mary Mother of God Hospital on a Monday morning at eleven-twenty. Please give twenty-four hours' notice if you wish to make a cancellation. I put the card in the things-to-do-or-take-notice-of pile.

Sugar Pea sits in her bouncy chair on the kitchen floor. I fill the wash-basket with wet clothes. Sometimes I wish her father were here; I wish Liam would come back and make everything all right, carrying all the answers in his pocket. *Put it out of your head, Jean.*

I have taken to hanging the clothes out instead of throwing them in the tumble-dryer, a habit I acquired on moving to Wicklow. Now I'm breaking it, in an effort to save the environment. Taking the basket out to the line, I am met by a fat magpie as it lands on the patio. They don't transfer from a distance very well; up close they look awkward, and the definition between the black, blue and white looks unreal. They look unnatural, like zebras: animals painted up for a parade. I salute the magpie, knowing it is a time to be cautious.

My energy leaves me as I reach the halfway mark on the washing line. I've had enough. My arms drop to my sides still holding a shirt, and I am suddenly drained. I drop to the ground and lie there. Turning over, I press my face into the grass. I breathe it in. Stretching my arms out, I flatten myself, close my eyes and breathe. After a while of stillness, I am ready; I can do this, get up and do it.

Sugar Pea sits as I left her, watching the empty washing machine with its door swung open. She happily waits for whatever is next in store for her. She cannot exercise her will on her environment. She is dependent on me for everything, much more so than an ordinary baby. I am always conscious of her, trying to anticipate her needs. If she felt unwell, would I know? Has she been sitting in that position for too long? Are her clothes caught up behind her back? Does she want something just out of her field of vision?

I vary her activities throughout the day, tying bells to her ankles while she kicks about on the floor, or attaching a plastic bag to the buckle of her chair so it crinkles when her hand hits it. I aim to stimulate her. Although she doesn't cry, she can make sounds of urgency if she is very thirsty or distressed. And, on the rare occasions when she has had a pain, she managed to let out a single cry. This reassures me. I bend down and give her a squashy kiss; her arms and legs gently wave about. *What do you want, Sugar Pea?*

∗

Trying to think of something nice to bring to Carol and Matt to say thank you, I consider a pineapple. Pineapples look like happy fruit; they look like they belong in colouring books with clowns and circus animals, in plastic packs with ten crayons. For a while, everyone was giving helium-filled balloons. Everything gets its space in time.

'Is she OK? What did they say?' Carol asks.

'She's fine... Well, for now, it's hard to tell. They don't really know what happened to her.'

'What did they say?'

'Not much, really. They said to keep an eye on her and follow up with the appointment the health nurse organised. I got it this morning; it's not for six weeks, so they mustn't think there's anything to worry about. Well, she's OK now...' I shrug helplessly.

'You must be really worried.'

'Yes, but they don't seem to be – and they're supposed to know what they're doing, right?'

'Definitely; if they thought it was serious, they wouldn't have let her out. They wouldn't take the chance,' Carol says with conviction. She bends down to Sugar Pea, taking hold of her and rubbing her arm she as did that night. 'Hello, Sugar Pea. You're going to be fine, aren't you? You must have got an awful fright, you poor little thing.' Sugar Pea sticks the tip of her tongue out and waves her arms about, with her wrists bent downwards and her fingers spread out like fans. One eye crosses and she makes us laugh.

Carol turns back to me. 'Matt was telling his mother about what happened, and she told him about a time in her childhood – there was a kid living down the road who every so often would take a turn and go blue, and they always put him in a bath of mustard. And it worked; it cured him every time.'

We look doubtfully at each other.

'Did she know what was wrong with the child?'

'No, but...' Carol's face turns red and she stops speaking abruptly. 'Oh, sorry, that was – I was thinking of something completely different. I was mixing it up with another thing,' she says quickly. 'It was someone else, years later, and it had nothing to do with... I'm sure Sugar Pea will be fine.' She takes hold of my arm. 'Really, I'm sure she'll be fine.'

My throat tightens. Sometimes unexpected concern hurts.

Once, when I was a child, I spent the night at the house of a friend of my mother's. The plan was for me to sleep on a cot in their baby's room, and they were to leave the door open so I wouldn't be afraid in the dark. I went to sleep, sufficiently pleased with the deal. When I woke up the door had been closed. I tried to stay calm and crept over to where I thought the door should be. Feeling around the wall, I found the door but couldn't find the handle. I was trying to keep quiet – I didn't want to wake the baby – but I had to get the door open. I held on to myself. I could see a chink of light coming from the window. There wasn't enough light to reach across the room and illuminate the handle on the door. With great care, I cupped what light there was with both hands to bring it over to the door; but every time, before I got halfway across, it disappeared. I tried again and again, but I just couldn't hold on to the light. Then it all got too much for me, the fear took me over, I panicked and started banging with my fists – 'Open the door, open the door!'

Suddenly the door opened, and the lady grabbed me and hugged me and said, 'It's all right, you're all right now.' She stayed with me and put me back to bed. When I calmed down, she left, with the door more than halfway open and the light on in the hall. And I didn't wake the baby.

Tucking Sugar Pea into her cot, I stuff teddies between the mattress and the sides in an attempt to jam the blankets in. This way Sugar Pea might not kick them off during the night, leaving herself exposed to the elements. By some undetectable means, she manages to get out from under them as soon as you leave the room. If you watch, she waits until you leave, and she is particularly skilled at waiting. I don't feel I have the right to spy on her. She is entitled to her privacy, and that is fine by me. After tucking her in, I put on her musical mobile. I do the same thing every night. I want to give her a structure on which to map her world. I kiss her good night and leave her door slightly ajar.

Throwing myself down into the overgrown sofa, I look at the TV guide. I don't see anything worth watching. I have a restlessness inside me. I get up and check the books in the bedroom; nothing there grabs my interest, so I look in the fridge. I can't see anything I want; all the goodies are gone. I head to the attic to see if anything interesting is happening in the sky.

All the stars are where they should be. Nothing seems different from last night. The answers are out there, but they are hiding. I just can't see them. If I had been studying the stars for years, maybe I would be just about to stumble across an answer. I have wasted so much time.

I pick up a book and flick it open at random. 'Titan is the only moon in the solar system that has an atmosphere.' I flip the pages: 'A rotating neutron star sends out pulses of radio signals.' Again: 'For twenty years, from 1979 to 1999, Neptune was farther away from the sun than Pluto.'

I hear a noise, one that shouldn't be there. Dropping the book, I rush down the stairs, through the door, out the closet, to the right, past the bathroom and directly to her bed.

Sugar Pea looks startled; her eyes stare blankly, motionless. Her whole body is stiff, arms out at shoulder-level, legs dead straight, toes pointed. Her fists are knotted and her jaw is clenched.

With both hands, I shake her gently, urgently calling her: 'Sugar Pea, Sugar Pea!' It registers in her face. She recognises me and begins to collapse her muscles back into a normal state.

Then I see him sitting at the end of her cot. He's about the size of a cat. His eyes glint and he's grinning right at me, showing two long rows of small, pointed teeth. Human-ish. The terror starts at my toes, sweeping up at lightning speed, up my trunk, raising my arms up in the air, and I smash them back down on top of him. They go right through him, crushing the blankets. He's gone.

It wasn't real. I imagined him. That's what it was. It was the blankets. They were wrinkled up in just the right shape to look like something. He couldn't have been real – how could he? I imagined it. It was just an illusion.

I tremble violently, gathering myself together. He looked so real. Scooping up Sugar Pea, I rush out of the room. She will sleep with me tonight.

My eyes dart about, checking every inch of everything, for days, watching for shadows, my ears straining for unusual noises. I investigate all the corners of Sugar Pea's room, making sure the windows are locked, the curtains drawn, there's nothing behind the closet or under the bed. I think I should contact the house's owner, but what would I say – I think I saw something scary? It's totally irrational, but I can't help myself. If Sugar Pea is in a different room from me, I keep a running path to her open at all times, all doors opened wide and all obstacles removed. I am ready to be at her side should the slightest disturbance take place.

A week of disturbed sleep begins. It starts with Marion and her clan. After they move one of their dogs to a new part of the garden, he decides to protest by barking loudly and persistently through the night. Marion is very sympathetic; she understands completely. She explains her difficulties, the fact that she is a defenceless woman with only her kids to protect her when her husband isn't home. In a controlled voice, I remind her that I, too, am alone in a house at night with my daughter. The dog continues to bark for days. It's driving me to the edge. At two in the morning I'm pacing the house, ready to kill. I open a window at the front of the house and scream, as loudly as I can, 'Shut that damn dog up! There are people trying to sleep!' A half-hour later, the dog, unperturbed, barks and barks. I look up their name in the telephone book and call. On the ninth ring he answers.

'Could you please do something about your dog? I can't sleep and neither can my baby,' I snap.

There's a pause, then: 'Right, I'll take care of it.' And five minutes later it stops. So they can do something when they want to. I slip back into bed after checking on Sugar Pea, who is sleeping soundly.

Then comes the growling from the bathroom, like a dog or a grizzly bear. It turns out to be the thermostat failing, causing the boiler to reach the anger point of near-explosion – but not before it has me stiff with irrational fear in the middle of the night. The problem is solved by a well-directed thud to the face of the gauge. Sometimes it's better to face up to your fears, sometimes not.

The last disturbance comes a few days later. As I pass the bathroom, I hear a clattering sound, unlike the growling. I am carrying a bundle of freshly dried and folded clothes when I hear it and see something move out of the corner of my eye. I jump and drop the stack. Surveying the situation, I locate the source of the noise, under the bath. It immediately makes me think of It, at the end of Sugar Pea's cot.

I grip myself, not allowing myself to get carried away. *Jean, don't be such a baby.* The worst it could be is a crow or a cat that has found its way into the wall. Arming myself with a flat steel comb, I get ready to prise the bath panel out. I manage to wiggle the comb under the edge. My heart jumps as I anticipate the monsters of childhood leaping out. With one last push the panel pops open, and I spring back and out of the room as fast as I can.

After a few minutes, I tiptoe back in. The space under the bath is motionless and dark; only a musty smell creeps out. I edge up bit by bit and pull the panel to the side cautiously, so as not to be taken by surprise with my face so near. Taking the comb, I fling it into the darkest corner while making another hasty exit. Nothing moves. I come back; there's nothing there. Before I decide it was just one of those things, I notice a hole in the wall, beside the pipes.

Making a quick mental picture of the structure of the house, I realise where it goes. The hole leads to the one inaccessible part of the house: the crawl space under the stairs. It runs behind the bathroom and Sugar Pea's bedroom. This is where the noises come from when all else is still.

I find the closest thing to a piece of wood – a large, thin hardback cookbook – and I nail it to the wall by the four corners. Now, if there are any crows living in there, they won't get out in a hurry.

I cross it off the list. All holes leading to the unknown are covered. All noises are accounted for. Now all I need to do is get

Sugar Pea to a specialist – someone who can sort out what is wrong with her, once and for all. Maybe then she will start laughing and crying in accordance with the rules of growing babies.

5

I catch a glimpse of myself in a shop window. If you saw me and you didn't know me, you would think I was part of a family. If my dead twin were here, maybe none of this would have happened. We would have been a pair. I am happily out of the way. Now that I'm gone, no one will remember the one who took so much effort to silence, the one who couldn't contain herself.

I remember walking down the stairs, three flights of steps. I had on a summer dress, short socks and a pair of knickers on my head. I had wet my knickers and hidden them under the bed, but she found them. She called me to my room. I came running, not knowing what she wanted. She put them on my head and told me to walk down to the basement and put them in the wash.

She gathered my sisters as I approached the ground floor, telling them to laugh. 'Look at Jean,' she said, pointing. 'Look at Jean with her dirty knickers on her head.' All the way down the stairs, into the kitchen. 'Go on,' she said as I opened the door to the basement stairs. 'Everyone look at Jean,' she laughed. I stepped down the stairs holding on to the rail, down to the washing machine, where it ended. Everyone saw my shamed face. It was not to be mentioned again. It had never happened.

Dr Baculum places a finger on the bridge of her glasses and pushes them one half-centimetre up her nose. 'Now, what seems to be the problem?'

I fill her in on the history, making sure I don't miss a thing. All the while she looks seriously at Sugar Pea.

'Well, there's nothing to be overly worried about.' Her movements are quick and jerky; when she moves, she looks like an insect unfolding herself. She gives Sugar Pea an obligatory smile, then looks at me. 'We will have this sorted out in no time.'

'But what is it? What's wrong with her?' I ask.

'The thing to keep in mind is that we know how to deal with it.' She does not want to impart too much information to me. 'It would be difficult to explain. It's very complex.'

'This is my daughter we are talking about. I want to know what's wrong with her, regardless of how long and complicated the explanation is,' I state clearly.

'I'm afraid we can't tell you. We find that trying to label and categorise these things causes more difficulties than it solves.'

'I want to know what is wrong, what it means and what can be done about it. You must be able to give me some idea, an indication.' I begin to tremble with anger. I keep my voice steady and firm.

Her voice goes up an octave as her anger builds to match mine. 'We cannot explain it, we can only recognise it. We have seen cases similar to this before and we know how to treat it effectively.' She calms herself. 'There's nothing to worry about. I've never had a case that I couldn't get some satisfactory level of control over.' As she says this, someone towards the back of my head whispers: *Pride before a fall, pride before a fall, make her touch wood, her arm is on the wooden desk, there's material between the arm and the wood, it will have to do.*

'What does it mean?' I say once more. I can't make an enemy of this woman; I need her.

'We have too little information to know. Once again, what's important is that we know how to treat it.' Her face seals over. She begins to scribble on a piece of paper. 'Now, if you'll go with my assistant, he'll give you the necessary instructions and we'll see how we get along. I'll see you in another six weeks.'

I'm not coming back. This is not going to go on for another six weeks. It is totally unacceptable and we aren't going to be a part of it. It should be illegal to suffer below the age of eighteen.

I must not break down. How dare she – how dare they all? This is not good enough. One day Sugar Pea will laugh and cry. One day she will call me Mama. The assistant takes me to the drug dispensary. 'Take the sachet and dissolve the powder into exactly five millilitres of water – measure it with a syringe. Mix 1.75 millilitres into your daughter's food at eight a.m. and eight p.m. daily. If she vomits within an hour of taking it, repeat the dose. If she vomits an hour or more after taking it, don't. If you have any problems, ring me.'

'Are there any side effects?' I ask, brushing Sugar Pea's hair away from her forehead with my hand. I do this regularly, to remind Sugar Pea I am here and, at the same time, to remind others she is here.

'Well, like most things, it can have side effects, but I wouldn't expect there to be any. We use this medication a lot. Call us in a couple of weeks,' he says.

'What does it mean? What's happening to her?' I ask.

'Don't worry, they know what they're doing,' he answers.

I know he's trying to be kind, I know I shouldn't be angry at him, but I want him to get the fuck away from me. I take the medicine, manage to force out a thank-you and get the hell out of there.

The Buddha sits on the fireplace. I would have liked one in stone, but this was the best I could find. It was cast in clay and has an expression close to Sugar Pea's. I put a group of daisies and ferns to one side of it and light a beeswax candle on the other side. Lucky charms. I look forward to the day when I will look back and marvel at how we got through all this.

That evening I put on Sugar Pea's favourite pyjamas, the all-in-ones with a zip up the middle and soft brushed cotton on the inside. I've never understood pyjamas that were soft on the outside with ordinary textures inside. It seems to me they are designed with the parents in mind and not the child.

I give her the first dose of the drugs. She looks at me with large, open eyes. I know the drugs will not work for at least a week, but I search for changes anyway. I kiss her slowly. 'Sugar Pea, I love you. Tomorrow will be a better day. Good night, Sugar Pea.' She watches me for a moment longer, then lowers her eyelids.

Gravel may be great for crunching, but it isn't any good when it comes to pushing buggies. Before I can make my escape, I meet Betty, nodding and poking her paper at me. I take it. 'Thank you, I'll read it as soon as I get back home.' She goes off, happy with herself. Today she has saved another soul. I have succumbed. I'll leave it here till I get back and then put it in its place in the bin.

✳

Lifting a smooth ornamental stone, I am about to shove the newsletter under it when I am distracted by a glimpse of a little world beneath. There is a population of woodlice, spiders, slugs and an assortment of fungi. From city life to under-stone life, each microenvironment seems complete unto itself. Everything is in its place, whether it knows its place or not.

Betty's place in the community seems to be converting non-believers and keeping weary drivers alert to all possibilities. I didn't have Sugar Pea baptised. I know how much it goes against the grain to do that in a country where even non-believers baptise their children. It was believed, years ago, that children were open to all the evils of the world until they were baptised. People would keep vigil over an unbaptised child in case the fairies came and stole it and replaced it with one of their own. I suppose a child as unusual as Sugar Pea would have been looked on as a fairy child. I stop in the grey, wet road to look at Sugar Pea. She is pleased to see my face, as always. Her lower lip drops as though she is preparing to speak. She certainly has an elflike quality. Fairy or not, it doesn't matter to me: she is the one I want, she is the one I love.

In the good old days, we tortured sick and weakly children in the name of God. Our technology is better today; now we can spot them in the womb. 'Thank God I have you – thank God you came to me and not someone else.' We head to the shops; the leaves tumble along after, hurrying us along.

A red van passes us. Beware of vans. I watched Oprah talk about people disappearing, particularly women and children. I have taken the dire warnings seriously – beware of the unmarked van. Apparently, the van is the favoured vehicle used to abduct people. Beware of the van. The expert on abductions imprinted the message forever on my mind. Don't get into the van, at all costs. Once they have you in there and the door is shut, there is no going back. These are the critical moments, all or nothing, the fastest crossroads you'll ever come to. It's as well to be prepared.

Sugar Pea jumps; she looks like she thinks she's falling. The medicine isn't working.

I get home and put Betty's newsletter in the bin and park Sugar Pea in the middle of the hall. Immediately I begin to clear my bedroom of all electrical items – the television, the radio, the alarm clock, the lamp. There is too much electricity in the room. Electricity must be flying through every room in the house. As soon as all things electrical are banished from the bedroom, I get the packaging tape and seal over the sockets.

Clearing away the books, I reassign the space to Sugar Pea's bed. It feels like it took no time, but it must have required Sugar Pea to exercise her patience. Sometimes I find it hard to stop once I get going. I put all her blankets back on and rearrange her teddies. When I'm finished, it looks like her bed has always been there. And the only electrical thing left in the room is the light dangling from the ceiling.

She could be sensitive to electromagnetic fields – I vaguely remember hearing about that. Maybe they interfere with the electrochemical impulses in your brain. It's worth a try. I move on to the kitchen and read the ingredients on every jar, packet and bottle of baby food; I throw out anything containing dairy products and write a note to myself to get soya milk. Sugar Pea is nearly weaned off breast milk and has started on the cow, but this is the end of the cow for now. I write myself another note to find out if there are any masts serving the mobile telephone networks nearby.

She arrives, and I straighten my skirt and go to the door. The house is clean and Sugar Pea is as shiny as a new pin. The hospital contacted St Michael's House and they have sent out a home teacher for children with special needs. They're jumping the gun; it will be a temporary aid.

She comes bounding through the doorway like a great big floppy puppy with the largest eyeglasses ever seen. Brown curls bounce along, adding to the movement about her head and grinning face. She's at least six and a half feet tall, bursting with life, right out of her clothes. She greets me warmly, and as I lead her into the living room she is straight over to Sugar Pea, breaking the silence of the afternoon with a booming voice and a laugh that goes well with it.

Good God, who is this woman? I ask myself. A huge stripy bag is plonked down beside her; from it come all sorts of noises, an array of lights, beeps, honks and jingles. Sugar Pea jumps to attention, arms and legs in the air and excited tongue poking out of her mouth. She is as dazzled as I am. The woman sits straight in front of her and looks directly at her. Carefully, she slowly enunciates each word.

'Hello, Sugar Pea. You are beautiful. My name is Gráinne.'

I explain the name situation. Then I settle down to watch, noting how she interacts with Sugar Pea, and don't interfere. Without looking down from Sugar Pea's face, Gráinne reaches out to the side and slides the magic bag closer to her. Without even a glance, she produces a shiny, jingly turtle.

'Look, look.' She gently takes Sugar Pea's hand in her own and guides it over the turtle's back. She presses the oversized button with Sugar Pea's hand. 'Music,' she says, as the toy begins to play 'Old McDonald Had a Farm'.

She uses specific words for every action, and repeats them: look, nice, more, good girl. Presenting one object from the bag at a time, she waits until it's been fully explored, or until Sugar Pea loses interest, before she fishes out the next one. There are things to watch, textures to test out, sounds, music and little sample jars with handwritten labels – lemon, lavender, mint, vinegar – to smell. Everything has been collected and thought of in preparation for Sugar Pea.

Gráinne pauses in between activities and leaves it open for me to join in or not. 'You're the best,' she tells Sugar Pea. I have never seen anyone talk to Sugar Pea so directly and for so long. Sugar Pea is so excited she pushes her head forward, sticking her tongue out as far as it will go, and lets her eyes roll around in her head. I laugh at the sight of her looking like a character in a book of fairy tales. 'What are you like?' I ask her.

Gráinne looks at her and smiles. 'She's like herself,' she says.

With that remark, I make up my mind: I like her. In an hour's time Sugar Pea's head starts to tip to the side and her eyes shut down; she's had a long day and several jumps. She falls asleep before the class is over. Gráinne stays and chats, rubbing Sugar Pea's sleeping foot the whole while.

She suggests we apply to the Health Board for a chair, one specially designed for children with low muscle tone. She suggests that Sugar Pea could use some extra support around her trunk; her spine should be protected while she doesn't have the muscle tone to hold herself up. It could easily take six months to process the application.

'If it's important, I'll buy it myself – just tell me where to go.'

'Well, she'd have to be fitted for one – ideally in a seating clinic, where we would find the chair most suitable to Sugar Pea's needs.

You wouldn't really get it any faster by paying for it yourself; and she is entitled to it by law, just as she's entitled to a medical card. It could cost anything from fifteen hundred euros upwards.'

'Really? That much?' I wasn't expecting it to be that expensive – and I need to watch my money until I have an income again.

'I'll look into it and see how fast we can get Sugar Pea into a seating clinic.' She kisses her on top of the head and gathers her stuff from the floor. As soon as the stripy bag is off the ground, it begins to hoot and flash lights.

I thank her and tell her not to worry. Secretly I know that by then Sugar Pea will be better and have her strength back. We'll give it to another child who needs it while they are waiting for theirs.

Eventually Gráinne makes a move for the door and I show her out. I am delighted with the meeting. I feel the session went well, and it'll be great for Sugar Pea while she needs it, but I'm drained from the duration of social contact. Saying goodbye, Gráinne heads for her car, squeaking and beeping all the way.

As I close the door, I feel as tired as Sugar Pea. Turning into the living-room doorway, I'm jolted out of my sleepiness. I see him.

He is sitting on Sugar Pea's chest, at her warm, open mouth. He's sniggering and hissing; his hideous yellow nails scissor and recklessly fly about in front of her face. She lies there completely defenceless. His black shadow cuts across her lightly flushed cheeks as she sleeps. My stomach plummets as I surge forward, shouting, 'Nooooooo!' He savours the moment and takes a marked look at me before he plunges through her soft flesh, straight to her centre, and shakes her with phenomenal violence from within, lifting her up off the ground. He's inside her. She seizes up, her face frozen in terror; her eyes open, wide and unseeing. Her lips pull back over her clenched teeth. Her body is rigid.

The room explodes. 'Sugar Pea, Sugar Pea!' Frantically, I gather her stiff body to me, trying to make contact, repeating her name, rubbing her face. She can't hear me. She lets out a painful wail followed by whimpering moans. He trembles uncontrollably inside her. Her whole body jumps, shaking. Then she collapses in my arms, dazed and limp.

I try to enclose her. I would slit myself open if I could take her inside me. I see a flicker come back into her eyes. She remains limp; she's drained. We stay there, sitting on the floor, rocking in despair, unable to think or do anything.

There is nowhere to turn. I know how well madness fits me. It would never be believed. They would tear us apart. I would rather have us die together than leave her in this world without me.

The razor had been designed with safety in mind. It didn't break easily. Bending the plastic rim back, I exposed the blade. I sat on the toilet and bent over my ankle. One quick swipe: that was all it needed. I stared in amazement as the thick layers of skin slid open with precision. They had been waiting to be opened. It was far deeper than I'd meant. I hadn't thought it would slice so easily. I could see the tendons leading to my toes, and a forked vein. Then came the gush. The blood spurted everywhere. My stomach dropped. *Oh my God, what have I done? I need help. I'm in big trouble now.*

The blood slowed to a thick, steady stream. I knew I had to do something, fast. I flung the twisted razor behind the toilet and half-ran, half-hopped out of the bathroom, down the hall and into the kitchen. I spotted a knife on the table; it didn't look sharp enough, but I panicked and wiped it in the blood anyway, threw it on the floor and raced, hopping, to the living room, where they were all watching TV. 'Mammy.'

The doctor stitched the edges back together while trying to make me laugh. It was funny how little it hurt. The neighbour who had driven me there drove me back home. She thanked him and closed the door.

'What did you do?' she screamed.

'The knife fell on my foot,' I said.

'You're a liar. What's this, then?' She held up the razor between her long, yellowed nails. 'We found it behind the toilet. Now tell me what you did!' Her screams flew through me. 'Your bed is still warm. You got up out of your bed and did it yourself, with this razor. Isn't that what happened?' she shrieked. 'Look what you've done to your sisters. They've been crying the whole time you were gone. Don't you care?'

I balanced on one leg. I looked at the floor.

'Do you want me to take you to a psychiatrist? Is that what you want? To be locked up in a madhouse and get electric shocks in your brain? Because that's what will happen to you!' Her screams faded into the distance. 'Do you know that?' The stitches were itching me.

I was glad to get into bed, with my foot sewn up. It was over. I watched a boy get beaten up in a film; even though they didn't touch his head, blood spilt from his mouth. My sister explained it to me. The blood came from his mouth to demonstrate that his insides were injured. I hadn't meant to cut so deeply. I had only wanted to collect the blood, in case I needed it as a sort of proof. Now it was proof against me. I could be sent to the madhouse. I had to contain myself.

*

Just when I think I'd rather die, I see the sun on her hands. I am pushing Sugar Pea's buggy along, looking over her from behind; all I can see of her is her hair, her hands and her booted feet. Then the sunlight comes speckling through the trees, landing in sparkles on her fingers. Her hands are close together in front of her, wide open, with each finger spread out; and slowly she moves them in and out, tilting them this way and that, a random dance coming together with the dappled light. It is so incredibly beautiful that, all at once, I feel everything is right in the world.

I look forward to the day when I can talk to Sugar Pea and share ideas. Without language, there doesn't seem to be any satisfactory way to enter into her head or invite her into mine. I can't imagine what it's like to think with no words. How would you formulate ideas and string them together? How could you file an idea and retrieve it, without a word to attach it to? How can I know and feel what it is to be Sugar Pea if she never has the language to tell me? She is in a different living space, one I cannot experience.

But I am projecting down the line about things that will never happen. She'll talk, of course she will – just later than others. Smushing my forehead up to hers, I try to send a calming brain-wave to her. I repeat my mantra in my head. I will it to enter her. *Oingggggg, oingggggg* – the sound that lingers in the bell after it's been rung. It was given to me when I was eighteen and in the Transcendental Mediation Centre in Dublin.

We go back to Dr Baculum. She reassures us it is completely normal for the first drug not to work. We are not to worry. I'm ready to change one drug for another. It's the only real way to get through it: attack from all angles, and something will work. I take the prescription and leave. Time is passing by and Sugar Pea is stuck.

On the way out, we pass a girl in a wheelchair. All her limbs are directed to the right; even her eyeballs look to the right. The thing that really strikes me is the air around her face. More and more, I see beauty in the faces of children with difficult lives. It must have always been there, I just didn't notice before.

I make eye contact and smile at the girl. In the lift down, my head resonates and I'm reminded of the great depression I had in '96, when life turned black and little people in my head kept jumping off cliffs.

On the return journey, Sugar Pea and I stop at a hardware shop. I scour the shelves for evil-thing-living-under-the-bath poison, but there is none to be found. I settle for the extra-large box of rat poison. I spot a few rat-traps at the counter and throw them in for added attack power. I will cover all fronts in this war. Whatever it is, we will stamp it off the earth. I march out to the car with a new determination. Sugar Pea enjoys the bounce in my step as she sits on my hip; I have her clutched in one arm, with the poison in the other, and the drugs in the car.

Prising the bath panel open, I scatter half the box under the bath, making sure to fling it into each corner. Then, using the claw on the claw hammer – and realising now why it's called a claw hammer – I prise off the book nailed over the hole and shove the rest of the rat poison through, box and all. Everything reeks beneath the bath, and the walls are encrusted in mildew. I replace the book, nail it in place, set the traps and close up the panel. If there's anything alive in there, it will be dead soon. Even the innocent will go down if it means fixing Sugar Pea.

✳

I sit on the sofa with Sugar Pea smack up against me – body-to-body contact. I have a book on astrophysics on the other side. I tap out a tune with my pen on her belly button. She turns away and pretends not to notice, only to turn back for more when I stop. If the game takes too long to start again, she flings her leg at me, then turns back to wait again. It is vitally important to keep contact with her. If she has nothing to see or feel, then her inner space might as well be in outer space. I trace her features with my finger before turning the page. Gravitational forces act between all masses. There is a force acting between every person and everything else in the universe, between me and the person sitting next to me. The gravitational pull draws us together with the strength of one millionth of a neutron.

The death of a super-giant star is so violent, particles created in a supernova explosion will hit the Earth's atmosphere. Changes in life on Earth can occur because of cosmic rays from supernovas exploding thousands of light-years away. Maybe I should keep Sugar Pea indoors more.

6

I hope she doesn't have a girl. That would make a huge difference. There would be no comparisons. I hope it's a boy. That would be much easier than having a little girl living on a plot next to our plot, going to the miniature primary school when it should be Sugar Pea. Maybe Sugar Pea will catch up, and I won't have to see a tiny baby crawling past her (twice the baby's size) as she lies helpless on a blanket on the floor and watches.

It's the clothes that bother me. I don't know what to do about the clothes. No one is going to wear Sugar Pea's clothes. I don't like lying. I'm not comfortable with it. I don't mind the lies that we all tell, like saying we're delighted to see someone when we aren't or 'I'll give you a call.' These are acceptable lies. They help life flow, taking the edges off.

The problem is the lies one level up. *No, I don't have her old clothes, I gave them away. I forgot to wash them and they all went mouldy. I left them out on the line and Marion's dogs ate them.* When Carol first told me she was pregnant, I told her I was happy for her, and I tried to be. She was so excited, but I knew something was bothering me right away. A sense of dread entered me; something wasn't the way it was supposed to be. Now I know what it was: it was the clothes.

I don't want to see somebody else's first steps, her reactions to a magpie in the garden. I don't want to see a little girl exploring the world and chatting happily. I don't want to see Sugar Pea's clothes crawling, then walking, without her. I won't mention the clothes to Carol, I won't offer. She won't ask.

Two appointments arrive. The expected one is from Gráinne, who now comes roughly once every fortnight, and the other one is from the hospital. It is addressed to Sugar Daly. If I knew who this Sugar Daly was, I might pass on the message.

Reaching into the waxed paper, I pull out two slices of bread. There is a yellow dust, not mould, on the first few slices. There is something living in the bread. I throw the loaf in the bin and take two slices from the freezer to toast. The house is cold; I like the heat, but I couldn't have gone through that much oil already. Sugar Pea's still asleep – what a lazy girl.

The heating is housed in the dusty shed at the bottom of the garden, waiting to be investigated. I search for the red press-me-and-all-will-be-well button, checking out all the ups and downs and underneaths of the furnace. There is no sign of a button or switch, which is just as well, because the temptation to flick or push it, regardless of the consequences, would have been too great to fight. It might have resulted in me blowing myself and the shed out beyond the Earth's atmosphere while Sugar Pea slept soundly in her bed.

I push aside a few bits and pieces that have somehow ended up living under the boiler. There might be a manual, a leaflet on what to do when the heating fails, that was left by some organised mind and has found its way under the furnace. I pull out a stick of metal. Sticks of any sort remind me to beware of the stick. They are not to be trusted. A stick could easily be an insect camouflaged to look like a stick – and they are remarkably good at it; I have been fooled before. But it's worse to find the stick that resembles the insect that looks exactly like a stick. You waste a lot of time giving it quick pokes and jumping back, only to feel foolish on finding out it's just a stick.

This stick is fine; there's no imitating cold metal. I poke around. The only thing left under there is a tin of odd-shaped, unidentified engine bits. I use both hands to shove it to one side and reveal the final corner. There is something there that gives way if poked. Mid-poke, it occurs to me that it could be a nest of sorts; but nothing stirs. So I retrieve it slowly, careful not to break it up or knock it off the stick.

It's a dead, mummified hare, squashed fairly flat and still intact. It is easily identified. Its eyes are wide open, whether from fear at the point of death or from the skin drawing back as it dried, I have no way of telling. The most striking thing about it is its mouth. Seen in profile, it appears to be in mid-scream – a long-drawn-out silent scream, from the point of death on into infinity.

There are no clues to how it died and what made it scream such a scream. I wonder where the scream went; if it goes on forever, where does it travel? It could be possible that having the right receptors would mean you could pick up screams millions of years later, like light seen from stars that exploded billions of years ago. I lift the hare up on the garden spade and put it into the bin. I don't suppose it would make much difference to a mummified hare whether it decays in the soil or in a dump. At least I heard its scream.

Matt told me the history of the red bricks of the patio. They came from the nearby psychiatric hospital; when they tore down one of the old buildings, a few years back, they let the local people drive up and take away as many bricks as they wanted. Government bodies are like rivers – they always take the route of least resistance – so they collected their allocated funds when in need of money, and didn't bother to sell the bricks in a market where old bricks cost more than new.

The owner of this house realised the value of old red bricks and collected his share, so Matt said. I seized the opportunity to enquire after the owner; however, Matt had never met him either – he heard this from a local gardener who had collected a few himself. It was last summer when I received this information from Matt; since then, when all things are silent and it's sunny enough to sit out for a while, I sit on the patio and listen for the wails and the howls that I imagine must have been absorbed by such a porous material as red brick. The psychiatric hospital would have been called an asylum, amongst many other names, at the height of its use, when four and a half thousand patients were buried in a field with no name, all rolled into one.

I can't remember which came first – the noises, or being told of the bricks' origins. I didn't say anything about the sounds to Matt when he told me about the bricks, but I can't use this as a marker: if I'd been familiar with them already, I would have been sufficiently wise not to mention them. There have been plenty of times when I didn't know what to say, but there are more things on the do-not-say-under-any-circumstances list. Listening to and empathising with red bricks definitely falls into this category. So much anguish to seep into the walls... I lean down and run my fingers along the bricks.

✳

The heating is working again. I notice the floor needs a good clean. Gráinne will be coming over in one hour and fifteen minutes; countdown time. I'd better vacuum. I plug the vacuum into the electric socket closest to the centre of the house – this way I can race from room to room without stopping.

Balls of dust have gathered and floated about on the hard floors. They have nothing to catch them, so they float with every breeze made by the movement of a door or a body passing by. Their journeys come to an end in corners, where they stay until they are vacuumed up or until a gust of wind greater than average sweeps them on their way, dust bunnies. I seek them out, sucking them up. Maybe there are too many dust bunnies in the house. The mummified hare could be a sign: eradicate the bunnies and Sugar Pea will be fine. She's allergic to dust, she has an extreme reaction to dust.

I sit and wait, Sugar Pea sits and waits, both of us silent. I watch tiny particles, disturbed by the flurry of movement on the dust-bunny hunt, floating in a ray of light. They float, we breathe them in.

It is between the pieces of air that I feel my sister's presences. Staring in quiet moments. I don't mind her coming, feeling her creep up my back or run a finger along my neck. Sometimes she gets annoyed and plucks hairs from my head, one by one, for all the hairs she never grew. I sit still while she does this. I have matter and she has none. Sometimes she expands throughout the entire room, breathing in all the air, creating a vacuum and leaving me without a breath. Why did I dare live when she did not?

'How's my favourite little girl?' Gráinne arrives, jiggling, beeping and honking.

'She's waiting for you. Gráinne, I heard Sugar Pea say "Mama",' I tell her excitedly. 'It was just the once, but it was definitely "Mama".'

Her face halts; her mouth opens but she doesn't say anything. I see straight away it's silly. A child unable to babble, unable even to smile, couldn't have said 'Mama'. How embarrassing: I have blurted out a wish disguised as a belief, a hope with no basis in reality. Gráinne doesn't say anything; her expression says it for her. She knows it's impossible. I decide to let it go; I will let her know another time that I know. As much as she doesn't want to say it, I don't want to hear it. I don't need to be told. Sugar Pea has communication problems between her head and the rest of her. I do too. Sometimes words with sharp edges cut my throat and I can't get them out. So they embed themselves there in a knot. I can't think of anything to say.

'You know, I meant to warn you about the ditch in the village, just in case you decide to stop in there some time,' I say.

'Really? What's that about?' asks Gráinne, picking up on the opportunity to change the subject.

'This ditch is a big hazard. It's across the road from the pub called The Slaughtered Lamb, and it's at such an angle, you would have no idea it was there until you were in it. It has no ledges to mark it out. So don't try and park there, because before you know it you'll be in it.'

'That's incredible. Would they not think of putting up a warning sign?' she says.

'I don't know if they've thought of it or not, but even if they did, I'd say they wouldn't put one up. In the summer, when all the locals drink out front at the picnic tables, I think the ditch provides their only form of entertainment. They have great fun watching outsiders pulling up close enough that it looks like they might fall in. In fact, I've seen the odd bet being made on whether cars will go in or not.'

'Well, I wouldn't like it to be said I'd spoilt their fun,' laughs Gráinne. 'They don't sound like the sort of people you would want to mess with.'

'No, they're not that bad. If there was a woman on her own or elderly people or children in the car, they'd point out the ditch. But I did hear that, when someone actually does fall in, most of the people watching jump up and cheer – as though they're watching a football match. And it's talked about for weeks after,' I say, as Gráinne laughs more and more. I am encouraged by her enjoyment. 'They love it, especially if the people in the car have a funny accent – or don't speak English at all.'

It's odd to be the one who can make someone else laugh, who feels comfortable chatting freely. I can't pin down at what point in life I lost comfort in myself and awkwardness set in. One minute I was running freely through the air, well able to think and move without any body awareness, up a tree and over a wall; the next I was grounded, pulled back into my skin. It was shortly after that I began to leave it behind purposely.

In school, I found myself with a tendency to watch others. *They are my classmates,* I would say; but the girls did things I didn't do, they spoke in high-pitched voices and gathered in flighty gangs. The boys shouted and jostled for position. I found one quiet friend amongst them. We used to sit together in every class we could. I liked the way he smelt and we were comfortable in our closeness. We tried to 'go with' each other for a week or two, but it didn't work out. Basically, I wouldn't 'give him his bit'. He was looking for a girl with a looser sort of nature, and I wasn't the sort to change my sort to suit another. He provided me with a comfort and an interesting smell. I don't know what it was, but he got from me something he couldn't get from others.

I was stimulated by the story of a man who had found an extraordinary solution to a life he didn't fit into. He appeared to be in a state of unconsciousness, and everyone thought he was and let him be. Years later, it turned out he had created an entirely separate existence in his head; when he found his life in the real world was more than he could bear or less than he could be, he moved. He moved in his head to the other life.

Immediately, I started practising all the details in preparation for the move. It had to be real enough to step into. An error such as a gap in the floor could prove fatal. I decided I'd resemble Lindsey Wagner. I picked a home in sunny California, on the beach; a house on stilts ten feet high. It was an open-plan, single-storied house where everything could be taken in with a single glance. My job was to save people – I hadn't worked out who or what I was saving them from. I also had a rather vague group of friends and a boyfriend, but his face never managed to take on a more human quality than that of a mannequin. The problem with trying to establish an alternative life in your head is the constant interruptions. I would be just about to come to a conclusion about an essential detail when I would be interrupted, in school, at home, everywhere. I had to give it up before I managed to make the crossover. It got too unmanageable to live in two places at once.

It has been my observation that couples and people who don't visually fit together often end up going their separate ways. I am starting to appear shabby next to Sugar Pea; if I don't do something now, we won't look like we belong together. I'd better go shopping before our appointment.

A piece of paper crumpled in the letterbox catches my eye. It's a page torn out of a book. There is no indication of the title of the book or where it came from.

> *Changeling – A wizened or sickly fairy child put in place of a stolen human child. Unbaptised children were particularly vulnerable. Various methods were used to get rid of such a creature, such as thrusting a red-hot poker down its throat, roasting it on an open fire or abandoning it in a wood. The child would be safe if it was of God's making.*

'Unbaptised' is highlighted in red. It could only be Betty. How dare that stupid bitch? I should report her for harassment. I should throw her on a fire. I crumple up the page and throw it on the floor.

There's a bang in the living room; I jump. Sugar Pea knocked the box of baby wipes off the sofa onto the wooden floor.

Before we manage to put the boundaries of the village behind us, I take a bend and the road grates with loose chippings as I turn the corner. Holding the road, I see, just within my field of vision, something leaping out in front of us, something dark and flapping. Re-gripping the steering-wheel, I brake hard. There is no bang. I look up cautiously. It's Betty, standing and nodding and grinning. Her head wobbles around as though it's on a spring. Sugar Pea's head is forward on her chest.

'Jesus bloody Christ, you're bloody lucky I didn't kill you!'

I stretch back and push Sugar Pea's head back into the headrest of her car seat. Betty is totally oblivious to the accident that almost smashed her. She's edging her way around the car, delighted with her successful stop. I roll down the window.

'Get away from the car,' I roar, as my blood rises within me. I am so angry with her for causing this. She could be dead, and Sugar Pea probably has whiplash. I should have just run over her.

She backs up into the hawthorn hedge and raises her hand in a feeble wave as I drive off and away, accelerating loudly to express my anger.

By the time we get to Dublin, the anger has subsided. She's probably a bit mad and can't help it. But she'd bloody well better stay away from Sugar Pea.

There is a knack to balancing a buggy on a moving step, and I have it. On the way up the escalator you position the front wheels in the centre of the rising step, then lift the back end of the buggy in the air to make everything level. I go to the children's department first. I am about to decode the sizing system for the perfect baby dress when I notice a commotion coming from the homewares department. It is a one-woman commotion; she is on her own, digging through a mountain of cushions and flinging them about as she discards each of them for a better one. She is bent over, with her butt in the air and just her two arms coming out as they fling away cushions. She looks like a mole digging a tunnel. There is something familiar about that butt.

She straightens up and holds one of the cushions up in the air between finger and thumb. She inspects it. It's her. It's my mother. I duck behind a rail of clothes and peek out. My heart jumps against my ribs. It's definitely her, rummaging through cushions. And I'm definitely not coming out from behind this clothes-rail.

She stays there long enough for me to get a cramp in my knees and become concerned about our hospital appointment. There is no way out without passing under her nose. Grey particles shoot out from her towards us, bombarding our atmosphere. I shrink further back into the children's section. I wait; she leaves without a cushion, trundling down the escalator. How can a person put so much energy and disgust into choosing a cushion and then leave without one? Hers is an endless search for something that can never meet her criteria or subdue her fury. She has replaced me with inanimate objects. She has replaced me with cushions.

I wonder about my siblings, and how easily they accepted my disappearance. Where was their voice, their memory, their sense of what happened to me? I can't imagine not standing up for one of them, if it had happened to them. I can't imagine sharing my life with the perpetrator rather than the one who was perpetrated against. It doesn't make sense to me – but then, nothing ever has. Everything runs more smoothly if I am not there, painfully indicating that things are not as they all pretend they are.

It is easier to retain a whole set of beliefs than to accept the one that falsifies them. I was the falsification of the apparently happy family. I have to remember that it is their mother I am talking about, and to acknowledge me would be to acknowledge the cruelty of their mother and bring them closer to where I am. An imperfect mother is better than a cruel one, and a cruel one is better than no mother at all. If I am the problem, then the solution is easy. Still, just as they have difficulty taking the imaginary leap into what it might be like to be me, I find it hard to imagine what it is like to be one of them.

It is harder to reason out my mother. Why didn't I turn into her, or her into me? How horrible it must be to find that one of your children brings out all the worst things in you. Where did it come from, the grain, the turn in direction that made the difference between us? Maybe it sprang from the earth, in a quiet moment lying in the grass, or sprinkled down into my eyes as I faced the shifting sky on a rhythmic swing. Or maybe it was the whole problem: I was just too different from her. Whatever the truth of it, it supplied me with a secret plan. I knew that when I grew up I was going to have my own family, and it was not going to be like this one. My family would be different, and my child would never be made to feel the way I did. I would wait it out. I knew someday I'd start all over again.

We enter the Particularly Difficult Paediatric Cases department. I sit on the emotional edge of the bench with the others. This is not like entering motherhood, where everyone welcomes you; nobody wants to be here. We are all unified in our separateness, waiting for the day when we will no longer be a part of this. The only goal is out.

Dr Baculum arrives, orbited by medical-student moonlets. Sugar Pea is going to try her third drug. I am not an entomologist, but I suspect Dr Baculum's enthusiasm for the case of Sugar Pea Daly has waned just a bit. She has changed tactic. Somewhere along the line we have moved from 'not to worry' to 'this is more serious than we thought'.

I choose not to pick up on this, because I'm trying to read Sugar Pea's chart upside down. I make out 'global developmental delay', a suitably descriptive term – and it implies something late, not something that won't be coming at all. That would be called 'global developmental cancellation'. I want to tell Dr Baculum that I'd like to see Sugar Pea's chart, but this urge is counteracted by a strong desire to flee. No one can help us now. Just give me the next set of drugs and I'll be on my way.

Of course, this all goes completely over Sugar Pea's head. She is sitting in the buggy making happy sounds, little clicking noises in her throat. She is delighted with so many faces to look at; she sees the best in everyone. They all stare so sympathetically, but I don't want their sympathy, we don't need it.

Dr Baculum writes the prescription. They don't know exactly how these drugs work, or, for that matter, what is wrong. But third time lucky. I have decided that this will be the one that works.

Moving out of the building, I make my way towards the part of town where I know my mother would never go. Now I can be just a part of the crowd again. Now I'm just a mother with her child, shopping in the city. I take my time choosing Sugar Pea the prettiest and most expensive dress I can find, with tights and shoes to match. It is so expensive it's a sin. There are people in the world with nothing to eat, but there is nothing I can do about it. I don't give a damn.

What if she never walks or talks? How will I know her? How will I understand her? How can I do what is right for her if I don't know how she feels? Time is moving on and there is no first word. We are stuck on page thirty-six in *Child Development* and have no way of moving forward. How will I know her? How will we share our ideas?

I can walk into a bookshop and step inside the head of someone I'll never know, but I can't step inside my Sugar Pea's head. I can only hold her and look into her until the last attack releases her and she can see me and know she's not alone. Sugar Pea is a closed book, a life of silent pictures. Where does that leave her? How can I not project myself onto her, with no voice from her to tell me otherwise? Her life as a mirror?

The weather is bad; the wind is blowing thorny words towards my head from all directions. They are coming up from the ground, flying down the streets between the people and bombarding me. I've used too many words. I've used up all the language, too many thoughts and too many words; there is nothing left for her. I've eaten all her words.

The days go by while we wait. I watch for a sign that this is the third-time-lucky medication.

In the mini-supermarket we pick up drinking chocolate, dishwasher tablets and puréed fruit. It's the especially friendly cashier; she always makes room for Sugar Pea. The odd time, I see the man who owns the shop, the friend of Sugar Pea's father, and I wonder for a millisecond and then just as quickly shut that unwanted wonder out.

I greet the cashier.

'How's Sugar Pea?' she asks.

'Great – she's doing really well.' I angle the buggy so they can see each other face to face.

'Well, hello there, Sugar Pea. Are you shopping with your mammy?'

I search through my wallet for the correct change. I need to get rid of some; it ends up in piles around the house, taking up space. If you let it go unchecked it will eventually fill the entire house.

'How old is she now?' the cashier girl asks.

Before I can reply, I hear him sneering – I think it's a sneer. I can feel his dreaded presence. I can see by Sugar Pea that he's here. He's inside her. I drop my purse on the counter, rushing around to her, putting my face to hers. I take hold of her face. I frantically begin to talk her through it. 'It's OK, it's OK, Sugar Pea. I'm here.

I love you.' I let my hair fall down around us, forming a curtain, giving us some privacy in our pain. Her face is dark and contorted unnaturally, her teeth set, her legs rigid; she howls out in terror.

When the worst of it is over, I keep my hand cupped to her face, telling her I'm still there. My other hand pays and takes my belongings while this hand stays with her. I don't see or hear anyone else now. I push the buggy forward with my body, away from the counter, and move straight into the nearest corner, where we can gather ourselves.

I don't look at the people. I already know what they're doing. Most pretend they didn't notice the wail, the flying limbs. Some people stare; children look confused and frightened. There are no boundaries here. There is nothing sacred.

'What are you, a retard?' my mother whispered harshly, giving my ankle a discreet sideways kick – we were in public. Then she reefed me out of the shop. 'Now stand there and don't move an inch, do you hear me? Why do you always have to embarrass me? Acting like that – Jesus Christ. Do you know that woman thought you were retarded, making those stupid noises? I can't go anywhere with you but you make a holy show of me. What is wrong with you? Are you retarded, Jean, are you? Now stay there and try and act like you're not a bloody retard.'

With a final pinch to the inside of my arm, she went back into the shop. I pulled my sleeve back into place and looked at my feet and then around me. I didn't know what it was, the thing that was wrong with me, or even where it was, so I couldn't tell her. It was a puzzle. An old man smoking a cigarette against the wall was watching me; then he looked down.

'I was making funny noises,' I volunteered. He looked up

again. 'The lady in front of me smiled and said, "You poor little thing."' He didn't answer, so I looked for shapes in the sparkles of the granite walls of the shop-front.

If only Sugar Pea would put her fingers in her ears and make funny noises, if only she weren't in pain, I would put my fingers in my own ears and make them with her. Walking back through the village, I grip the handle of the buggy tightly for fear I might float away. Sugar Pea falls asleep. So what if you're different, if you're happy and healthy? Who the hell cares? Who decides how many degrees of difference are too many? What's so important about not standing out? I promise that, if this ever stops, I will let Sugar Pea be whoever it is she is. I swear I will never impose on her my subjective views of how to be in this world. Just make it stop.

'Jean, Jean.' *Shit*. It's Carol, calling from one of the picnic tables outside The Slaughtered Lamb. She waves me over.

Just keep going. No, I'll stop. No, I'll keep going.

'Jean,' she calls again. I had better make the effort. Sugar Pea will sleep for ages. I had better stop; it'll be OK. Step 1: indicate acknowledgement, and approach. I give her a wave and weave between the tables with the buggy.

'Come and sit down and have a drink with us. This is Camille, and this is Fiona.' They look like Carol-type people; they probably all went to school together and have remained friends ever since. I look at Sugar Pea, in a deep sleep.

Step 2: say hello and make introductions. 'Hi, I'm Jean.' I offer a hand to shake. 'And this is Sugar Pea, sleeping away here.' They move to get a better look at her.

'Oh, she's gorgeous,' says Camille.

'She's so sweet, I'd like to take a bite out of her,' squeals Fiona.

91

'Will you have a beer, Jean? I'm just going up to the bar,' asks Carol as she moves to go.

Step 3: sit down. 'Yes, please; that would be great, Carol,' I reply, and settle into position with Sugar Pea's face out of the sun.

'Isn't it brill that Carol and Matt are having one of their own? Those two will make fantastic parents, don't you think?' asks Camille.

'Yes,' I reply. 'It'll be really exciting for them.'

'I can't wait to have a little baby,' Fiona squeals, scrunching up her face again.

Carol returns with the drinks. As she nears the table there is a sudden upsurge in the noise level. We all turn to see what the cause is. It is coming from the roadside. Carol, standing with the four drinks braced between her two hands, spots it first.

'It's a car – it's parking at the ditch.'

We all stand up. By now everyone is trying to get a better view; some people are even climbing onto the picnic tables. A sturdy-looking couple in a red hatchback with a German reg are attempting to park their car. They edge closer to the ditch, not realising what awaits them. As they reach the point of no return, it's the luggage on the roof-rack that tips the balance – and into the ditch they go, with only the red arse of the hatchback left sticking out. A cheer goes up into the air.

But it's the pitch of the woman's scream, a scream of pure terror flung out in every direction, that drains the blood from several faces and sends pints of beer flying. And she screamed, not because she or her German husband was hurt; she screamed because, when she opened her eyes, she didn't see the mud of the ditch or weeds pressed against the windscreen. What she saw was Betty's dead eyes staring back at her, pressed up against the window, in the ditch where she had lain for several days.

7

On Earth, we always see the same side of the moon. The moon turns on its axis every 27.3 days, precisely the same time it takes to orbit the Earth. The other side of the moon never shows its face. The moon doesn't radiate any light of its own; it reflects the light of the sun on its surface of white dust. Very little is as it first appears.

When we walk between the sun and the moon, they look to be of similar sizes; but, due to an unusual coincidence, the moon is four hundred times smaller than the sun, and this is compensated for by the fact that it is also four hundred times closer to the Earth.

Of course, it's not size that counts, it's mass – mass being the factor with the most influence when it comes to gravitational forces. The sun may only be four hundred times the size of the moon, but it has 99.8 per cent of the mass of the whole of our solar system; that's why we revolve around it and not it around us. We hold the moon in orbit by mass and the second factor of gravity, proximity.

It's our proximity and density that exert our great influence. Density, to me, does not relate to a person's intellectual abilities. Density means greater mass in a compacted area, more brain per square centimetre, more thought processes. It could be that, like the sun, our densest minds are also the brightest. I like to think of myself as a reasonably dense person.

I was surprised to learn she had a husband; I had never seen her with anyone, not once. She was in the ditch for days, long enough to wash away the slashes of bright-red lipstick and the painted-on eyebrows. And yet there wasn't anybody looking for her, not even her husband. He claims she often went missing, and he had long suspected she'd join the Christian Revival group, who live banded together in a house. Somehow, I doubt he even noticed she was gone. I wouldn't suspect him of any foul play, on account of his obvious lack of interest.

I get ready to go to the funeral. I am driven by the thought of there being only one or two people in the church, as though she didn't matter in the end. I wear the right amount of black – black trousers, shoes and jacket with a patterned shirt – and I dress Sugar Pea in her ordinary clothes. The mass is at ten, so if I time it right, I'll walk down, arrive at half-ten, and just go to the grave-side behind the church.

Positioning Sugar Pea on the bed, I place her head on my lap to brush her teeth. Poking a little finger into the side of her cheek, I open up her mouth and start on the top row; I brush it from back to front, then the bottom row from back to front, and then move to the other side of her mouth. Sugar Pea gags on the tooth-brush with only three-quarters of her mouth done. Quickly, I remove the brush and lift her into an upright position to give her the chance to catch hold of herself. It's too late: she gags until she brings her breakfast up, all over herself, the bed and me.

'Jesus Christ, Sugar Pea, can't you do anything? Is it too much to ask you to swallow?' I jump up from the bed, pacing back and forth; I'm so full of anger, I want to strike her. I want to take her and shake her. I dig my nails as hard as I can into my palms and stop in front of her. 'For fuck's sake! I mean, really, is it too much to swallow the goddamned toothpaste when you can't even spit?' I clench my fist. This is too much for me, it's not fair, it's fucking ridiculous. I could kill her, I could kill everything. I look upwards and, with all the venom I can muster, I shout, 'Fuck you!' If there is a God, I want him to hear. 'Fuck you, you son of a stupid bitch!' I charge over to the wall and kick it as hard as I can until my foot breaks through the plaster. Then I take my raging fists and bang them against my head over and over. I hate this world, I hate this life, I hate everything.

After a few moments, I hear her movements; she sounds the same as always. Nothing makes any difference. I refuse to look at her.

I go through the motions of cleaning up the mess. I am conscious of how I handle her; it's not her fault, but I don't want to look at her. I just need some time. I put her in her chair in the kitchen and go and sit down in the living room on my own. I leave the two doors open but I can't see her.

Now we won't make the graveside; it'll be over by the time we get down there. I'm relieved in one way – I don't have to go – but, in another way, I was mentally prepared to go. I might have had a quick moment in the church to see if I felt anything – a presence or an atmosphere, some evidence of something willing to listen and able to do something. No, I'm glad. I don't have to go. I don't care about shoulds or coulds. I have a legitimate reason not to go out into the world today.

*

If I had known my grandmother – if she had been nicer to my mother, not forcing her to run and live as far as away as possible and only return after her death – then maybe my grandmother would be up there with my sister, watching over us and looking out for Sugar Pea. I cover the hole in the bedroom wall. I make a little wish. Sometimes they float off, looking for a home; most times they break and land at my feet.

Dreams of a room come to me, a place. It has two walls and a floor. They are more beautiful than can be expressed, more beautiful than can cross over from a dream to a waking state in any more detail than a sense of it. They form a corner – just the walls and the floor; there is no ceiling. There are no edges, they merge into the sky and the sea. It's the corner of the world. Where everything lost is found.

The heat comes in at the end of July. Sugar Pea and I lie out in the garden, her half of the blanket in the shade and mine in full sun. We hold hands where the shade meets the light, our faces to the sky.

The sun goes in behind a cloud, taking away some of the heat but giving us a good view of the clouds backed by the sun's intense rays. The edges of the clouds roll and wave as they push forward in the sky, churning from the outside to the centre. If you watch the edges and nothing else, they pull you along with them until you feel yourself ready to tip off the earth and fall up into the clouds.

It could be an entrance into another dimension, a different level of life, if you let yourself go with it. I could do it, just tip off the earth. But it's too unfamiliar, and I don't know if I could take Sugar Pea with me.

Maybe that's how people go over the edge. Their need to know is so great that they let themselves go beyond the point of no return. I'm a stop-just-a-foot-or-two-before-the-edge person, yet forever drawn to it.

I often find myself running through the house at night, banging off obstacles to get to her. It sounds like a scream in reverse, as though, instead of screaming out, she screams inwards, sucking in until her lungs can hold no more. I get to her, to let her know she is not alone. I use any means to pierce through the cloud in her eyes, talking frantically into her ears, making promises I can't keep and rubbing her everywhere to bring her back. When she comes back, she always takes great comfort in knowing I'm there, and I take great comfort in this, too.

Lately I see signs in everything. It's a sure sign you're on to something when suddenly you are bombarded with coincidences, signs and sequences. If pride comes before a fall, what comes before a rise? The clock says 12.34 and 56 seconds, and I see faces in the shadows and highlights on the carpet pile.

I study everything, keep my eyes open and my ears keen. The solution is here somewhere; when it passes I'll be ready to grab it. It'll be the thought flying through the air I catch, the one that no one knew was coming.

Today I have faith, yesterday I didn't. Today I believe that persevering with a whole heart will bring us what we need. I visualise her walking, running up to me with her little naked body and dancing steps in her feet. She hops at random between the steps; her eyes turn into sickle moons because her smile is so big it pushes up her cheeks, squashing her eyes. She says 'Mama' and points to the magpie: 'Birdie.' And she holds my hand as we walk, not briskly but at a toddler's pace, along the ditches, where hundreds of years ago a child just like her must have walked with her mother.

That is when I dare to look beyond my only true goal, which is to see the end of these attacks. I hear a scattering noise upstairs and instinctively look up at the ceiling window, where I think I see a movement; but I can never be sure. Entire worlds could live just beyond the corners of our eyes. There is no point going up there. I know there will be nothing to be found.

When Sugar Pea starts to crawl, I'll have to put a grid over the window in the attic floor that looks down into this room. I have no idea what weight it could bear, but I'm not about to find out. I'd hate to think what would happen if we fell through it and ended up not in the living room but somewhere else.

Buzzzz, buzzzz. I jump out of my thinking, causing Sugar Pea to jump. It's a normal jump for a normal reason.

It is her chair. It was scheduled to arrive this morning – a wheelchair for Baby. Sugar Pea's head isn't talking to her feet, and until it learns how, something has to be done.

You would never think there was such a thing as a wheelchair for babies. I have never heard anyone ask, 'What do you do for a living?' and get the reply, 'I make wheelchairs for babies.' The chair is heavy; it is made to last until she is seven years old. It is made to last longer than she will need it. It's very colourful, and I imagine it looks great in catalogues for baby wheelchairs, but it's going to clash with everything she wears. I will have to dye the cover.

It has two sets of wheels, indoor and outdoor. The whole thing weighs about the same as a Mini and is so big that either we'll be mistaken for miniature people against it, or onlookers will think something has gone seriously wrong with their sense of perspective. It is great to have a chair that hugs itself to you and brings you up to everyone else's level. No longer will Sugar Pea be at the mercy of crazed marauding dogs and car exhausts. It's so big we could run over stray cows. We will have to watch that we don't gather such momentum that we won't stop till we hit the next town.

The dogs are barking again. I rang up last night; the answering machine asked me what I wanted. 'Could you please do something about your dogs?' It didn't reply. Tonight they're barking again, and in the morning the noise will be replaced by the raging sound of his motorbike grating on my nerves. I ring up again to tell the answering machine to do something about the dogs, but it doesn't seem very interested. I can't imagine a more maddening sound than dogs barking through the night. Sometimes I get the impression they aren't barking in a haphazard way, but are actually barking at my house.

There aren't any more definite, absolute, one-hundred-per-cent-sure noises from under the bath. It is more a case of hearing a sudden bang or a creeping noise, but as soon as you pull your hair back and stick your ear out to focus your attention on it, it stops. If I think I hear something moving, I freeze, but it can wait longer than I can. It can wait unreasonable lengths of time. It out-waits me, and the very moment I give up is the moment I hear it move again. That is, if I am really hearing anything in the first place.

And that is the way it is in the wall where Sugar Pea's bed used to be. The crows must have moved out or died. A crow isn't cunning enough to move just the odd time or when you are just out of earshot.

The steel comb lies exactly where I threw it. I filed a visual memory of any distinct patterns of blue poisonous pellets I could make out, and they don't seem to have been disturbed. The only thing that bothers me is the fact that the underside of the book keeps coming away from the wall. The gap isn't large enough to let a cat through, unless it flattens itself down and creeps under the edge of the book. It would nearly have to seep out. The gap is no true indicator of whether something is in there or not. It could be caused by a change of pressure from a door slamming in an unexpected gust of wind. The thing to remember is that it is all very explainable and that I should not get overexcited by it. Each time I check it, I give the book a quick bang with the hammer and slam the panel shut.

When I use the bathroom now, I always leave the door wide open, even if it is cold. I'm always ready to dash out if necessary. My bathrobe hangs beside the front door, in case an unnecessary dash leaves me standing naked with someone at the door.

Picking up Sugar Pea, I bring her into the kitchen for her bath in the sink. The first water always has a funny smell, so I run the tap. Then I fold a towel over the edge of the sink to make it more comfortable for her. I support her head and back on my arm, firmly holding her arm on the opposite side. She is particularly difficult to hold when wet. She's a wet and soapy, slippery-as-a-fish little girl with limbs that can fly out at random.

There is only the swishing of the water to be heard in the silence of the morning. Then I hear the gravel crunching, fulfilling its function as guard gravel. The crunching is at the front of the house, so I wait for the doorbell. Instead, the crunching comes around to the side of the house; it reaches the back and approaches the door. It's Carol. She sees me through the window and comes in.

'What are you washing Sugar Pea in the sink for?' she asks, her face flushed with the effort of carrying her baby around.

'It's just handier than the bath,' I say, as I hold Sugar Pea awkwardly. I realise, through my awkwardness, that I actually don't mind Carol dropping in unexpectedly.

'Would it not be easier with all the extra room in the bath?' she laughs. She leans her elbows on the counter and then decides to stand up, leaning slightly backwards and holding her belly, instead.

'No, she'd end up floating all over the place and I'd probably have a broken back by the end of it.'

'Well, I just came over to check that you're not trying to get out of tonight, are you?' She inspects my face for any signs I might try and make up excuses to get out of it.

'No,' I say, as if I haven't been making up excuses since I moved here. 'I'm going out.'

'Well, I still think I should have been the first one to babysit Sugar Pea. Shouldn't I, Sugar Pea?'

'And you would have been, but then I wouldn't be able to go out with you, would I?'

'I suppose not, but you should have let me babysit ages ago.'

'Will you take my watch off for me? It's getting wet,' I ask.

'You're not worried about leaving Sugar Pea, are you?' She takes my watch off and leaves it on the counter; beads of water sparkle on the silver strap.

'No, I'll be fine. Sure, we're only going down the road; and I trust Gráinne. She loves Sugar Pea.'

'Right, then, I'll see you later. Bye, Sugar Pea. Don't you worry; your Auntie Carol will mind you the next time.' She bends over and kisses her wet face.

I wash her dead skin cells away. Each cell holds her genes, copies of my genes and those of my mother. Each cell makes up the instructions for her unique self. Changeling genes; perhaps they came from me.

The body renews its cells once every seven years. It's hard to think where the self must live in a system like this. I must find out if there are any cells that stay with you from birth to death. Hair doesn't, neither do teeth; I have no idea about bones.

Sugar Pea enjoys the water flowing over her as I pour it from a height. Her hair is back off her face and drops of water cling to her eyelashes. She looks more and more like a little fairy, a little changeling. She looks happily at me with an open mouth. I scrunch up her cheeks with my free hand to make her lips pucker like a fishy's. I kiss her fishy lips. She soaks it in.

Wash away, wash away, wash away. I want to be new and shiny.

I go back to the sink later to get my watch. It's gone. I can't find it anywhere. I look all around the counters and the floor, and check my pockets, but it's nowhere to be seen. I'm sure it'll turn up; I must have picked it up without thinking, or Carol could have.

I keep an eye on everything, searching for changes that shouldn't be there. On waking up in the morning, I check to see if anything has moved during the night. I am well used to scanning rooms for changes. As a child, I tried to find any piece of evidence that dolls really did have a life of their own. I'd line things up carefully, to make them impossible to put back exactly the same way if they were moved. And I'd make promises in whispers: if they showed themselves to me, showed themselves to be alive, I would be good to them.

I believe in Sugar Pea. I hold her head for her and wonder what it's like to have to have your head held for you. I arrange myself in a position that Sugar Pea often takes up, to get a feel of what it might be like to be her. I look to see what she can see and feel. I stretch my upper back and head as far as they go. This odd position that she takes up, I take up. There have been times when I've had expressions or done actions that I recognise as other people's. I feel like they have come over me and somehow I am them for that moment. I might accidentally make a comment just like a person I know would, or use a mannerism belonging to another, and at that precise time I feel like I have a sense of what it is to be them. I manage to find a stretch, one I know to be hers.

At times I try to go the other way and detach myself from her, knowing this could all end in an unimaginable event. She didn't come with a guarantee. If only I knew where it would all end, it might be easier to endure. Will she even make it to three in such a volatile condition, let alone walk or talk? Will she even live? How much can one small child tolerate?

'Where's Sugar Pea?' Gráinne arrives, arms open wide and eager for her.

'She's already in bed.'

'Oh.' She looks disappointed.

'Sorry, she was really tired. I couldn't keep her awake.' Shit, I should have let Gráinne put her to bed. I am taking no chances of disrupting her routine.

'Ahhh. Can I just have a peek at her?'

'Of course.' I motion her to follow, and we both stand transfixed by Sugar Pea's sleeping face.

'She looks completely peaceful,' whispers Gráinne.

I think it best not to mention the evil thing that lives about us; I realise that it must live somewhere between my fears and the actuality of Sugar Pea's attacks. The thing is that, if I knew that something was really living in the house, I could do something about it. I could get out. But it's difficult to know what reality is when reality has been denied all your life. You have to feel your way through a shifting existence, searching for something solid, seeking facts to hang your thoughts on. You just get on with it. I have my feet on the ground, my toes dug into the soil; there will be no floating off for me.

Carol and I go to The Slaughtered Lamb. It feels odd to enter the pub at night, after so long. I feel out of context. I feel the eyes and the nudges. We order our drinks and sit down. I'll drink carefully; I don't want to get tipsy when Carol is keeping her alcohol consumption down to the odd glass of wine during her pregnancy. I have to watch my drink anyway; I am easily affected by alcohol, and I certainly don't want to lose a good sense of myself.

'Well, it's about time you let someone mind Sugar Pea and came out,' says Carol.

'Yeah, I know. I'm glad I did.' I start to relax.

'I had this really weird dream last night. I dreamed I had the baby and I was holding her in my arms – except I was really tall, about the size of a two-story building, and I had her in my arms and I dropped her. Because I was so tall, I could see her falling for ages, and I thought I would die when she landed, but I couldn't do anything to stop it. And you won't believe what happened.'

'What?' I ask.

'She bounced as soon as she hit the ground, right back up into my arms. Isn't that so cool?'

'Yeah,' I laugh. 'A baby that always bounces back would be pretty handy.'

'So did you have any weird dreams when you were pregnant?' she asks.

'Loads of them, especially towards the end. I was dreaming

nearly every night that I was giving birth, and something strange would be connected to either me, her, or the birth. You know the way in the last trimester it feels like it's never going to happen.'

'Definitely. Tell me one of the dreams,' she urges.

'I dreamed I had just given birth to her and I was admiring her little naked body, thinking she was a miracle, and then suddenly she started to give birth herself. A little baby came out of her, and then the little baby gave birth to an even smaller one, and each new baby kept producing an even smaller one until they were so tiny you couldn't even see them.'

'That is just so cool. I'd love to always have dreams like that, or at least remember the ones I do have,' says Carol.

'Yeah, or forget them!' I laugh.

Carol hesitates. 'Hey, do you believe in premonition dreams? I'm a bit sceptical, but I wonder if the fact that I always dream about girls means anything. Not so much like we can see into the future, but more like your body already knows it's a girl and so automatically dreams of girls.'

'That could be true. Some parts of us know more about what's going on inside our bodies than we're conscious of – like the immune system goes to war before we have any idea that something's invaded,' I say.

'What about premonition dreams – do you believe in them?' she asks.

'No, not really, but sometimes I have dreams – like there was one where I was walking down the street and I saw this woman sitting in a coffee-shop window, and as I passed she looked out at me and raised the cup to her mouth, and then it was over. Then a few days later I was in town, and I suddenly realised it was the same street as in my dream – and in a part of town I had never been in before. So I turned towards where the coffee shop should be, and there she was, the same woman, drinking...well, I don't know if it was coffee or not, but I suppose I didn't know in the dream either. Anyway, it was the same woman, with the same cup raised to her mouth.'

'So you believe you can see into the future?' she asks.

'No, not really, not like anything big or significant; maybe just the small things. Maybe things that don't really matter,' I say.

'You know, I'm glad I got to know you,' Carol says, smiling. 'You're a really hard person to get to know; you can really keep your guard up.'

'I suppose I am.' My throat contracts a fraction, and I'm suddenly aware again of being in a public place. I had forgotten myself. I change the subject. 'I was reading a book called *Perception* earlier today, and there's a small part of the retina in the back of the eye that has by far the most acute vision. It's called the fovea. It has the greatest number of receptors and ganglion cells – the ganglion cells send information to parts of the brain to interpret what it is you're seeing. Anyway, if the rest of the eye had the same number of receptors and ganglion cells as the fovea does, then just one of your eyeballs would have to be the same size as your whole head. Can you imagine that?'

Carol laughs, only this time she looks a bit perplexed. 'Yeah, you'd look strange all right.' I know this description doesn't take into account where the ganglion cells travel to – they eventually lead to the visual cortex, which would probably need to be as large as the whole body, and then where would everything else go? – but I don't mention this as it would only complicate matters.

We spot the big fella, Michael, looking our way. I nod at him in a neutral manner. He makes a joke with the lads and hitches up his pants in preparation for making his way over to us. Normally, I would be happy enough to see him, but only passing by. Family noises can usually be heard from his home, which he shares with four sturdy-looking boys. He has lived without a partner since his wife upped and left him in the middle of the night four years ago. She has never been seen since.

He often packs the boys into the car and takes them off on an outing on a Sunday afternoon. And squeals of laughter that turn to protests can be heard in the summer months as he hoses down all the children, and any other child who might be passing by. He has an intolerable habit of collecting all sorts of junk in his trailers and piling it up in every available scrap of space in the front, side and back gardens. The Christmas fairy lights stay on the house all year long, and he has a growing collection of garden ornaments placed strategically alongside the mountains of salvaged goods and trailers.

'Oh, shit, he's coming over,' says Carol from behind her glass, pretending to be focused on a really intense conversation with me in the hope that he will keep walking by.

He stops at our table and places both knuckles on the edge of it. 'Good evening, ladies. And what are you having?'

'We're fine, thanks, Michael. Have to go easy on the drink,' Carol says, patting her prominent belly.

'No, thank you, I'm fine too,' I say when he turns to me, and give him a quick smile. His eyes linger on me. I can tell he won't be easy to budge.

'So what's the craic, then, girls?' he says.

'We're just having a quiet chat,' I say, hoping he'll get the message, but he pulls over a chair and shouts to the barman for a pint. Carol doesn't say anything else; she's too nice to say anything.

'If you don't mind, Michael, I don't mean to be rude but we were actually discussing a private matter.' I'll be damned if I'm going to sit here all night and listen to him acting the cock.

'Well, then, I'll just be over there if you need me.' He licks his lips and winks at me. The waist of his trousers has slipped below his belly again; he hitches them up and puffs out his chest as he saunters back to the lads. And a few seconds later a burst of laughter erupts from the pack.

Carol and I decide to leave before closing time. As Carol departs for the bathroom, Michael seizes the opportunity to make one more impression.

'Listen here to me, if you ever get scared on your own in that house…' He lowers his head and hushes his voice with seriousness. 'You can call me, and I'll come and sort it out for ya.' He waits a drawn-out moment for his remark to settle on me. Then he straightens up and puffs out his chest, rocks back and forward on his feet just the once and, with a knowing eye, says, 'You know, an intruder or a bad sort hanging about.'

'Thank you, I will,' I say. There is a certain sort of man who loves nothing better than scaring a woman so he can be the one to save her. I don't give any sign of feeling in any way threatened.

He nods again and says, before he goes, 'Now don't forget that – you being all alone and that.'

We walk beside the ditches in the dark while the coldness makes its way into our bones. Carol gets her little flashlight on, after a good deal of fiddling with it, and lets the beam of light fly back and forth on the road with the swing of her arm. I keep my eyes on the ditches, watching out for flat Betty's eyes staring back or a mud-stained limb sticking out.

I picture Betty's cold, decaying body in the earth where she is now buried, with the rain seeping through from above. I don't want to be buried, and Sugar Pea will never be buried – no, not in the cold ground, to lie night after night freezing with no one to hold her and warm her. When Sugar Pea grows up, I'll make sure she knows I want to go out in flames and burn up my energy in one go – just my ashes on the Earth, and the smoke drifting off into the atmosphere.

8

A star is a shining example of balance. It is in complete equilibrium. It needs to be, in order to exist: the outward pressure of hot material inside the star must balance the inward pull of gravity, otherwise it will either explode or collapse in on itself. A star must maintain its status, neither expanding nor contracting.

Massive spinning stars are losing their balance all the time, collapsing into black holes or exploding. Our lives are so fragile; our entire sun could be turned instantly into gamma rays in the most powerful sort of explosion ever imagined.

A reason? There has to be a reason. Why would the answers be inside an ordinary person? Cause and effect. What if the answers fell through a hole in the sky and went to a place where navy handbags, silver watches and dead twin sisters live? The reason could be in a piece of dust, but which piece?

I dump the drawer full of Sugar Pea's clothes on my bed. I read every label on every article of clothing; if there are any man-made-fibre clothes, they are out. Only natural cotton will be worn from now on, on both of us and on the beds. And no tumble-drying at all. The static electricity in man-made fibres is probably discharging in bursts and interfering with the positive and negative charges in the atoms that make up Sugar Pea.

Filling a large black sack, I remove the suspect clothes and dump them in the now-disused front bedroom. The room stays still, with no perceptible changes, day after day. I should reread all the books. I made a mistake; Baby doesn't work.

Sugar Pea wakes up. She watches my face. She purposefully lifts her leg and flings it at me, looking for my attention. I pretend not to notice. She waits, turns away, turns back, picks up her leg and flings it again. She directs it haphazardly, digging it into me, ohhing and ahhing. I smile at her and tickle her under the chin and around her wobbly neck. Never has anyone smiled as much as this child makes me smile.

As soon as Michael spots me on the road, he begins to make his way over. I don't know why he has taken a shine to me; I have been nothing but discouraging. He must like a challenge. Hitching up his trousers, he tries to make it to the end of his drive before I make it past his house. We are both moving as fast as we can, while trying not to appear to. He is halfway down the drive when he sees he is not going to make it, so he calls out instead.

'I see you made it home all right, then?' he hollers after me. 'No intruders, then?'

'Yes, I did, thanks,' I shout back over my shoulder, keeping the pace up, flying down the road.

Michael has the biggest plot of ground around. His house has stood there since long before any of the other houses were built. His father sold most of the land that people eventually built on. I should ask him about the history of my house, only that would involve talking to such a degree that he might interpret it as interest in him. On the far side of Michael's house, he grows vegetables – big old cabbages with more holes than cabbage. Nothing looks particularly appetising. It all looks like it would need a good boil in a pot for several days to reach the stage where it could be consumed by anything higher up on the evolutionary scale than a pig.

There are a couple of rows of strawberries that don't seem to bear any fruit; this could be due to the boys picking every bit of red off the plants before it gets the chance to get any bigger. It also could be due to Michael's unusual manner of dealing with the threat of birds. This is to hang dead birds of various shapes and sizes from strings tied over the strawberry rows. I would have thought the sight of bird carcasses dangling in the breeze would have been enough to make even the strawberries stay away and refuse to grow at all. As strange a sight as it is, I do understand that country people have a different way of looking at things than those of us from the suburbs and cities. I try to hold myself back from judging some of the odder country ways. This is not always an easy task.

I think Michael's dream is to be a hero. He works as an unpaid volunteer in the fire department. He is trained and ready to go whenever they need him. At least, my perception of the matter is that he wants to be a hero; it could be that he enjoys playing with fire. Either way, being a hero is not trying to scare women into needing you, or creeping about at night hanging dead things from sticks.

In a universe where chaos and order are proportional to each other, perhaps the more order I try to impose on my life, the more chaos comes into it. At the same time, the more chaotic life becomes, the more inviting a sense of order is.

An ad catches my eye: 'Craniosacral therapy for children with special needs. The laying on of hands.' How far would I go with my theory that anything is worth a try? I'll put it aside; I may become desperate enough to try even the unworkable.

The darkness is falling; soon the little Halloween monsters will be collecting. Sugar Pea is fed and all set to go. I'll get her dressed up. We'll go over to Carol's and then head for the bonfire.

Before dressing Sugar Pea in her green flower-stalk clothes, I check her skin carefully for spots or blotches, any irregularity. But it appears to be fine. Our latest drug could have a severe side effect. If there is any sort of change in her skin, the drug has to be stopped immediately, and she has to be brought directly to hospital. In rare cases, it can cause every layer of skin to peel off the entire body.

She still looks fine. I tie the green strip of crêpe paper with yellow petals around her face. Her curiosity is stimulated; her eyes turn both ways as she tries to figure out what it is crinkling about her face. She may not know that she's a sunflower, but I'm sure she will enjoy all the attention and smiles she'll get.

Taking a cracked and redundant saucer, I put a few unwrapped sweets on it and soak them in a little of the drug with skin-peeling possibilities. I open the bath panel and put it down, in the hope that, if the drug doesn't work for Sugar Pea, it might at least poison the thing under the bath. I can feel the skin on my arms alert at the idea of going under the bath. The hairs on my arms stand up. The edge of the book is away from the wall again. A cold chill runs up my fingers and sends shivers through me, like a dull electrical current.

Buzzzz. I jump and bang my head off the underside of the bath.

The sweets scatter as I leap backwards. I realise it's only the door. *Buzzzz*. Little demons and witches are at the door. I lean the panel against the bath and stick my head out into the hall.

'Hang on, I'll be there in a minute.' I wash my hands as quickly as I can, while I keep an eye on the black space under the bath where the panel is not attached properly. *Buzzzz*. I don't even bother to check whose kids they are; I just fling sweets out and close the door as fast as I can. I go straight to the bathroom, where I snap the panel back into place. Then I let go of my held breath and lean back against the opposite wall. I remind myself that I have never actually seen anything under the bath. It is not confirmed that something lives under there.

A warm feeling spreads over the back of my hair. I put my fingers on it; it feels sticky. The red blood clots on my fingers. I feel nauseated. I slide down against the wall and look at the firmly replaced panel on the other side of the room.

It's only then that I see the teeth-marks around the edges of the black hole behind the toilet. I stare at the hole, trying to fit this new piece of information into the situation. It can't be seen from any other part of the bathroom, only from here on the floor where I am.

I shake my eyes clear. It's definitely there – a small hole in the skirting-board behind the toilet. The edges seem chewed, as though a rat gnawed it, or at least something with sharp teeth. I want to touch it to make sure it's not a hallucination. My hand stretches out, fingers coming closer to it, just to make sure it's real. Just before I reach it, I think I see a movement, a glint, a reflection of light.

I withdraw my hand and race out of there and grab the first book I see, the hammer and nails. One leap into the bathroom and I shove the book over the hole, pressing it as hard as I can with my foot while I get the nails in. *Buzzzz, buzzzz.* The door will have to wait. One last nail straight through Planet Neptune, the planet with the worst storms in the entire solar system.

Then I turn off the light and lock the door. I'm going to get out of here. I can't stand it any more. Rat, cat or evil substance, this house is driving me crazy.

I go to the front door. Marion's kids are standing there together. All the boys are covered in sheets, dressed as ghosts and ghouls. The girls are a mixture of witches and pop stars. I'm extra-nice to them, and give each one a good-sized helping of sweets from the bowl sitting just inside the door.

Sugar Pea the sunflower is in her chair, patiently waiting for her turn to have Halloween fun. And she will have fun. We'll get out of this house.

Think of the devil and it appears. Michael arrives at the door with his four boys, standing in a row, each trying to get his bag up the highest and the closest. Bags full, they race off; Michael gives me a nod and a wink from the side of his face.

I open the bathroom door an inch and turn on the light. Everything is the same. Again I remind myself that I haven't actually seen anything. A rat could have made the hole years ago, a rat that died a peaceful death in a field after leaving the house. Sugar Pea has attacks whether I see things or not. I will look for a new place to rent in the locality.

It's bitterly cold outside, as it always is on Halloween night; cold enough to freeze the tits off a witch. Matt answers the door.

'You made her a tulip,' he says.

'She's a sunflower,' I say with mock annoyance. 'Are you ready for the bonfire?'

'Um, I don't think we'll be going. Carol thinks she's started her labour.'

'Really? Is she all right?'

'Yeah, she's not really bad. But she wants to be on the safe side. Come in and see her.'

Carol is moving around, sorting out last-minute things. Her face keeps changing from excitement to worry and back.

'Are you all right? Your labour's started?' I ask.

'I'm not in any real pain yet. Hopefully I'll be one of those weird women who don't get any real pain and just sail through it,' she laughs, unconvinced. 'I'm getting contractions about once every twenty minutes. So I don't care if it's too early to go in, I'm not taking any chances. Especially after you practically had Sugar Pea in the car.'

'I did not. I had loads of time,' I laugh at her. 'No, you're right: it's better to be safe than sorry.' I give her a big hug and a kiss. 'Don't worry; it'll be over before you know it, and you'll have your baby.'

Pushing the buggy down the frosty driveway, I take in the clear night sky sparkling everywhere. If I turn to the right, I'll be home. I could sit in front of the fire and listen for noises. If I turn to the left, I'll be at the bonfire where all the neighbours are gathered. I wish I was more comfortable with others. I should have made a bigger effort.

I turn left and force myself to keep going. I can hear the noises of excitement and see the glow of the bonfire above the hedges. I can't turn back now; everyone will have seen me. Dragging the buggy up the rough patch of earth, I manage to find the only piece of land left that hasn't succumbed to the rain and become thick

116

sludgy muck. People are standing in little groups surrounding the fire.

I feel so stupid. I didn't keep up my New Year's resolution to integrate more fully into society. If only I hadn't overtaken so many buggies up and down the road. I should have stopped and said hello. But I heard the whispering as I passed. They spoke too early and too loud – loud enough that I knew they were talking about me, but not what they were saying. Sometimes I replied, just loud enough that they knew it was a reply but not what I was saying.

Relief comes in the form of the cash-register girl. She comes straight over to Sugar Pea and shows her a sparkler. And just after her, Michael appears. He has packets of sparklers and a crowd of small people following him wherever he goes, hoping to get hold of one.

'You'd better hope Betty's ghost isn't wandering the ditches,' says Michael.

'Oh, Michael, you're terrible, saying a thing like that – God forgive you,' says the cashier girl, laughing and looking at me with an 'isn't he awful' expression.

'Sure, wouldn't I protect ya if she came after ya, Clare?' Michael chuckles until he realises one of his boys is lashing into the bonfire with a stick twice his size and threatening to topple the whole thing over. 'Joe, Joe!' he shouts, and runs after him.

'Did you ever hear what happened to Betty?' I ask.

'Yeah, they thought it was a hit-and-run but, like, there were no bumps or anything. So I don't know – maybe she slipped into the ditch and broke her hip or something. Old people do that, you know.'

'And they don't know for sure what happened?' I ask.

'No, but I heard that her son came over from somewhere for the funeral and didn't even speak to the da. Just arrived for the funeral and said nothing to nobody, and then off he went.'

'She has a son?' I am surprised that she had not only a husband but children as well.

'Yeah. I don't know him; he doesn't live here. Me ma said that Betty went a bit funny in the head after a cot death. And then the da started on the drink. It was a little girl, I think – the cot death.'

'That's awful. Did she not get any help from anyone?' I ask.

'I don't know; I don't really know much about her, just what me ma said. I think the son's name is Liam or something – at least, that's what I think me ma said.' She doesn't notice my reaction; she is lighting another sparkler for Sugar Pea. I am transported into a different state of consciousness, my blood races through me. She said his name was Liam. Could it be *Liam*?

'I used to mind kids like Sugar Pea – you know, with special needs and that,' she says.

We stare at the sparkler spitting out tiny dashes of light in all directions, and the great flaming blades leaping out of the bonfire. So many faces in the flames. Could it really be Sugar Pea's father, and he came from a family like mine? The thing that frightened him was that he saw himself in me. At the same time, I am struck by the realisation that I had no time for Betty. She could have been Sugar Pea's grandmother, and I never knew. I overlooked her, disregarded her, and wrote her off because she was too many steps away from my world view. I didn't want to understand, didn't want to ask her questions or chat and be friendly and open, just because her perspective on life wasn't like mine. Her language was different. And now she's dead. There are too many questions without adding new ones, they are bombarding me, my brain is melting. *Concentrate on the fire, Jean, the flames.*

*

Water – that's the answer: there is something in the water. I'll use only bottled water. I'll make everything from scratch and I'll cook all her food in bottled water.

The house is still when we return; nothing has happened. I have to fix that hole properly and get my book back. I'll keep it on the coffee table, with the nail-holes in each corner, to remind me of my foolishness. Everything is locked up; we go to bed. I wonder how Carol is getting on.

I'm in a long, narrow, dark alley with Sugar Pea. It's heavily shadowed and dank. We come to a blackness so thick we dare not go through it. We start to turn back, only when we do, the exit is blocked by something rummaging in a pile of rubbish and making a hissing noise. I edge up quietly, as close to the far wall as possible, in the hope of passing unnoticed. Whatever I was looking for down the alley doesn't matter now; all I want is out.

Then it sees us. It's him. He looks up at us and his eyes spark with interest, and he sneers. He has found us. He looks at Sugar Pea and reaches his two hands up for her. Opening and closing them, with their long yellowed nails, he starts to say in a grating whisper, 'Gimme, gimme, gimme,' over and over again, as he speeds up towards us.

I back up, pulling Sugar Pea up higher and turning her away from him, on the opposite side of me. I search my pocket for anything to use as a weapon, but all I can find is a necklace with dangling sparkly letters attached. His eyes spot it and I can see he likes shiny things, and I throw it at him.

He stops and picks it up. He likes it and squeals, but what he really wants is Sugar Pea. The letter-charms flash and gleam as they drip between his fingers. His hands start to make grabbing motions again and he makes for Sugar Pea. There is nowhere to retreat except into the blackness.

'Gimme, gimme, gimme,' he hisses. He wants Sugar Pea; nothing else will do. We run into the dark.

With a stifled scream, I break through. I wake up. Quickly I check all around: he is nowhere to be seen. Sugar Pea is sleeping soundly. The room is still. It was only a dream. Thank God, it was only a dream. I shudder with utter dread as the thought hits me: he's been plucking strings of words, one by one, from Sugar Pea's mouth.

9

The leaves laugh in the trees. They are unperturbed by me. The earth moves on. It does not own my madness. She waits by me.

I have been fighting all my life. All those years ago, I climbed up on the sink to search in the mirror. I was looking for the future. Fine lines have started to branch out from my eyes. I am a long way from where I thought I would be.

Nothing has moved in the bathroom all night. Only the copper pipes and the radiator creak and groan with contractions and expansions as the heat drops and rises. The sink drain reeks of stagnant water. I run the tap until the smell disappears.

I should change sides. I'll be the evil one instead. I'll be the one scratching inside walls. I'll break into people's houses, find their sleeping babies, and suck their breath away.

'I want to make an enquiry about a friend. She went in last night. She was in labour,' I say.

'Just a moment, please, I'll put you through to the labour ward.'

It rings. I hope the baby's not a girl. 'I want to enquire about a Carol Walker.'

'Ms Walker is still in labour. Why don't you call back in a few hours?'

The motorbike is running again. Every day this week Marion's husband has started it and left it roaring for a good fifteen minutes. It adds nicely to the sound of barking dogs. I'll start searching for a new place this week.

Sugar Pea and I still have the business of Dr Baculum to attend to. There is a small blotch on Sugar Pea's forearm. To be more precise, I'm not sure if it can be classified as a blotch or if it's just a pimple. I stop the medication. The list of tried medications grows as the hope of one working diminishes. There are always craniosacral therapy and dolphin therapy to consider. We could never stop just short of the cure.

It is clear from the start that Dr Baculum regards this meeting as an opportunity to get rid of us. We are the difficult ones who refuse to be cured, a stain that will not go away. Rather than have her spotless record tarnished, she wants to be rid of us – rid of us before anyone can say she has failed. I suggest it might have been an idea to work our way through the list of medications at a quicker pace and arrive at this point sooner.

Indignation straightens Dr Baculum's back and a glare appears in her eyes; her angles sharpen. Now it won't be sufficient to wash us away. She suddenly hungers for revenge for my daring to suggest there might have been an alternative approach.

'The outlook is very, very poor,' she says. 'It's most distressing.'

I don't say anything.

'This must be the worst case I have ever seen,' she says. 'You know, I really don't know of any other child as bad as this,' she says.

She looks at me, but I'm not going to flinch for her. Her straight, blunt hair dangles on either side of her face.

'Oh, no, wait – there was one.' She raises one finger in the air, then brings it to her mouth. 'That's right – a boy; he was as bad.' She readies her tongue and shakes her head, and then, in a casual manner, she flips her hand and says, 'Oh, but he's dead.' She pretends to think back over it. 'That's right: he died from it. Now, is there anything you'd like to ask me?'

I do not blink, or twitch. I look at her blankly while she throws a dead child at me. She has nothing left to offer, and I walk out of the clinic for the last time.

She made me wear it. She knew it scratched me. It was red. It was all over me, up my arms, behind me. The red dress was crawling over my skin. Quickly, I pulled it off and flung it under the bed. My hands grabbed hold of a friendly blue plaid skirt, a bluey-green jumper and long navy socks with beautiful sparkly spirals. I jumped up off the floor ready for school.

'You look ridiculous. Put on the dress that I told you to wear,' she said very loudly.

'But, Mammy, I don't like that dress. It makes me itchy.'

'Stop whining and do what you're told,' she shouted, slamming the door. 'And hurry up.'

The spirals were sparkling on my legs. If you squinted your eyes and turned your legs back and forth, they looked like stars. Maybe I could still wear them; they were my favourites. They

123

came right up to my knees and stayed in place. I folded the skirt up neatly. It was the exact right size for the shelf; the bottom edge lined up perfectly with the shelf edge.

Kids laughing out on the road distracted me. It was some sort of game with a rope.

'What ya doing?' I shouted down to them.

'Mind your own business,' Mark, the bigger boy, yelled back.

'Bring us out scissors,' a smaller boy, who I didn't know, yelled.

'I don't have any,' I laughed, delighted that I had been given a request.

'Well, go find some.'

'OK.' All I needed was a pair of scissors and they'd have to let me play too.

I knew I'd better hurry. My jumper was stuck over my head, with my arms still in it, when I felt someone beside me. Afraid of being tickled by my little sister, I struggled to get out fast. Suddenly I felt pain shoot through my head, and I was reefed up off my feet and landed on the floor. Through the bluey-green jumper, I heard the window slam shut. I didn't know what had happened. Before I could get up and pull the jumper off, the shouting started. It came out of nowhere.

'Is this what you want – to learn the hard way? You're going to bloody well learn if it's the last thing I do,' she roared as she grabbed hold of the hair sticking out of my jumper and pulled me towards the door. I couldn't see. The shouting moved off into the distance. I couldn't see my feet as we reached the stairs. My socks slipped on the wooden steps and I went crashing forward with no arms, banging my legs and my side; my head was yanked painfully back as she gripped my hair in her unyielding fist. There was no time for me to think of all the different pains. I would think of them later. *Just keep your feet flat on the surfaces; you don't need to see.*

I realised where we were going when the must-smell hit me. A voice from inside me forced itself through my lips, through the bluey-green wool: 'No, Mammy, no – please, Mammy, no...'

'You should have thought of that before,' she hissed.

'No, please, Mammy –' I tried to hold on to my hair inside the jumper. I tried to pull back. I didn't want to go there. My body twisted and banged off things, edges, as we went underground to the basement. I was thrown out of the storm and in through the little door under the stairs. I got my head free and reached my hands out just before the door locked. Her footsteps rose above my head and the basement door closed.

Bruises can't kill you but black air can, sucking out your breath. I backed into the corner and scrunched myself up. The scary things seeped in from all sides. I waited. Maybe my twin would come and I wouldn't be by myself.

I keep feeling like I'm forgetting something, something important. If only I could see where it all comes from. I could follow the trail back and find the source. I could grab it by its tail, claw up its back and prise open its mouth. Maybe if I took twenty-five paces to the left, then turned to the right and clapped my hands. Sugar Pea has such trust and faith in me.

I stand on the stool in the attic and watch the full harvest moon floating brightly over the land. The day and night are equal. It's a good night to lose yourself between the layers of sparkly lights, with the villages below and the stars above.

The phone rings. 'Hello, Jean; this is Gráinne. Sorry to disturb you. I hope you're not busy.'

'No, I'm not. How are you?'

'I just rang to tell you there's a programme on in a few minutes about the interaction of children with special needs and their pets. I thought you might be interested,' she says.

'Their pets?'

'Yes, the way animals can tune in to children with special needs and sense different things about them.'

'Really? That sounds interesting,' I reply, half-interested.

'Well, I thought you'd like it. You have a cat, don't you?'

'God, no. Why would you think I have a cat?'

'I was sure I saw a cat curled up under Sugar Pea's cot when I was babysitting,' she says.

The room begins to turn. My hand drops the receiver. *Oh, God... Don't panic, just get out. Pick up the phone, say goodbye and get out.* 'I have to go now. There's someone at the door. I have to go. Thanks. Bye.' I put the phone down. He's real. We've got to get out.

I race down the stairs to the bedroom. Just as I reach the door, it slams in my face, stopping me in my tracks. Then, silently, it swings back open. The room is still and Sugar Pea is asleep in her cot, but the air hangs heavy and oppressive. I know he's here. Slowly I step over the line into the room. Step by step, I silently make my way over to Sugar Pea, while scanning the room.

A sickening wave of fear floods over me as I spot him above me, clinging to the blind, near the top of the wall. Charging over to Sugar Pea, I grab her in one great swoop and race for the door. He screeches, darting around the room. The air cracks and splits as the door slams shut, trapping us. I whirl around to face him. He is sitting on the edge of Sugar Pea's cot rail. His red eyes glint as he sneers. A glistening drop of drool falls in slow motion from between two sharp little teeth. My head is exploding. He smiles directly at me; then, in one great gasp, he sucks all of the air out of the room, right out of our lungs.

Gasping, I fall to my knees, clasping Sugar Pea to me. The need to survive with Sugar Pea is greater, and somehow I manage to lunge for the door and reef it open.

Clutching Sugar Pea, I grab my keys and wallet. *Here we go, Sugar Pea; it'll all be over soon.* I should have believed my eyes. I can't believe this might actually be the end of it all. I should have known – and, at the same time, I can't believe it's really true that he exists. It's supposed to be all in your head. But Gráinne saw him too.

I pull out of the drive and over the gravel with the sense of leaving it all behind. It's over.

10

We'll make plans tomorrow. We'll drive up and down the coast until we find the place for us. We need a brand-new house without a history, in a new estate, up for rent for the very first time. What I want is a truly suburban house with no voices left imprinted in the walls, only silence. I'll make a list. No dead crows hanging over strawberry patches or mobile-phone masts attached to primary schools.

There are too many words in the air from mobile phones and teletext and phone texts and radio signals and television signals; this is a planet full of words, flying through the air we breathe into our lungs. They probably pass straight through our skulls as we walk down the road. Just one communications satellite can relay a hundred thousand conversations in a day.

Maybe Sugar Pea will find her own words now that he is gone. will he sit on her chest plucking them from her mouth. of all the other children he may go in search of voices in the night.

We could move to Spain. What a great excuse that would be never to speak again. We could stop talking to everyone and live in a warm and comfortable silence, just Sugar Pea and I. If she can't join my world, I can join hers. All we would hear would be a murmur of a language we don't understand. Visions would pass before our eyes and we would be warm all year round, with at least three hundred days of cloudless sunshine. I'd smile at the Spanish people as I pushed Sugar Pea along the beachfront. Every night we'd fall asleep listening to the sounds of the sea. We could open a self-service bed-and-breakfast for people who found it too difficult to talk any more – people who found that so many words had become so tangled in their heads, it was beyond the point where they could be unravelled.

But then, we don't have to think along those lines any more: he is gone. We left him behind in Kilreadon. It's over now, and we have to think in new ways and plan for a different future. It's time to be happy. And yet I continue to jump, certain she is being attacked, only to find her calmly looking around. *It's OK, Jean, it's over,* I tell myself. Soon I'll be able to step off the edge.

We have been driving south for nearly an hour when a name draws us into a town. It's called By-the-Way. We follow the signs stemming off the main route. It's what we are looking for. We need a place to plan what to do next.

It looks like all of life has stood aside from this place and left little more than the structure of what used to be a town. It is a seaside resort, with all the eeriness of a place deserted to the cold, howling winter winds and ocean mist. It probably was full of sunshine and life-noises a few short months ago, but it's hard to imagine. The road that edges the sea is grey, and drizzle falls lightly from the sky.

There is not a person to be seen; the only evidence of life is the odd car parked at random down the strip. They are in assorted tones of murky colours, as though they're trying to merge into the scenery. It could be that the town has leached the colour from them.

The buildings look cracked and old. A small fairground stands still, partly covered in plastic sheeting, with most of the moveable bits tied down. The plastic flaps in the wind, and metal clangs upon metal relentlessly. I can't imagine finding much death in a town that appears to have died long ago. Dead things only turn up where there is life. We drive into the small parking lot of what was once a large seafront house but has since evolved into a B&B. It has more cars outside it than any of the other B&Bs: two. And it looks the most welcoming, in that it is at least open.

I enter the lobby with Sugar Pea bundled up in my arms; there is no one there. A Tiffany lamp stands at the end of the dark, elongated reception desk. It provides an indicator to where I am, rather than where the lamp itself is. I am at odds with the world but sufficiently receptive to take the glow of the lamp as warm and cosy in a turbulent environment. If my thoughts were nearing black, then the lamp would mean that the days are so dark, we have to turn lights on in the middle of them.

The sounds of 'I'm Just a Girl' play in the background. There is no bell to ring.

'Hello?' I call out, and wait. I sit Sugar Pea's bum on the desk to bear her weight.

A girl pops her head around a doorway behind the desk. 'Oh, hiya,' she says, and disappears; the music level drops in an instant and she reappears. 'Sorry about that – I didn't hear ya.'

I ask her if she has a room vacant. It seems like a ridiculous question, but she carefully checks the registration book all the same.

'Yes, we do. One room, is it? A single or a double?'

'Do the singles have double beds?' I ask.

'They do, yes.'

'I'll take a single, then.'

'How long will you be staying?'

'I'm not sure yet, but it'll be about a week, anyway.'

'I'll see which is the best room to put you in.' She goes through the list of possible rooms, mumbling to herself about defects that need to be righted. She must have been born here. She looks like she's in her late teens or early twenties, and this is not the sort of place you have ambitions to move to. I'd say her parents own the place, or she lives locally and she got the only job left in the town. Either way, she'll probably move on.

After juggling all the options in the book, she smiles. 'Tell you what – I'll give you one of the double rooms at the front of the house and only charge you for a single. How's that sound?' she asks.

'That sounds great. I'll take it. Thank you.'

'They're the nicest rooms, anyway, and they look right out over the beach.' She marks us in and closes the book.

It's only when I put Sugar Pea into her wheelchair and bump it backwards up the two steps into the lobby that I realise there is no wheelchair access. There's no lift up to the bedrooms. The receptionist isn't sure what to do. The chair is too heavy and awkward to carry up and down the stairs.

'Have you someplace I can store it at ground level, and I'll carry her up?' Already her lack of muscle tone can make her feel considerably heavier than she is.

'You can leave it at the bottom of the stairs, if you like,' she suggests.

'I'll really need something more secure than that. It's worth over two thousand euros, and our world would grow considerably smaller without it.' Thank God it was beside the car when we left.

'I can put it in the office behind the desk. Will that be OK?'

'That will be great. I can just go in and get it when I need it.'

One landing up, before the stair turns, there is an alcove cut into the wall and a peeling statue of the Virgin Mary. On the second landing, there is a huge bouquet of peachy-pink and pale minty-green fabric flowers on a thin-legged table.

The floorboards groan and grate as we enter the room. I sit with Sugar Pea while inspecting the room with my eyes alone. There is a disconcerting smell of must. The bed is hard and indifferent to us; it doesn't know us. Beds always take a while to get to know you. The molecules that make up the bed and the molecules that make up you create a lot of friction on first meeting and must sort out their differences before they can settle down and sleep side by side.

I have formed close bonds with my pillows over the years. When I was young, I would sit with my legs folded and hug my pillow with both arms wrapped around it. I would rock to the edge of tipping over. Your awareness becomes balance, edges and varying angles. There is no you, just motion.

I can't imagine us getting anywhere here; we can't even get up the stairs with Sugar Pea's chair. The clouds grow weary and the drizzle stops. After getting her chair from the office and setting off down the road, we come to a shop. We are halfway through the doorway when it becomes apparent that the rear wheels are spaced wider apart than the front ones and they aren't going through. I wiggle the chair and tilt it to the side, but there's no going through. If it doesn't fit, then it doesn't fit, no matter how absurd it seems.

The red-faced shopkeeper spots our predicament and suggests I leave Sugar Pea outside.

'No, I wouldn't like to leave a child outside on her own.'

'Stay there, then, and I'll bring what you want out to you,' she shouts.

'No, thanks very much – it's not important,' I say, reefing the front of the chair out of the door and manoeuvring it about in one great swing.

'Are you sure, now?' she yells after me.

'Yes, thanks all the same.' I'll be damned if I'm going to stand outside a shop shouting my requirements, and even more damned if I'm going to leave her on her own at the mercy of chance events on the paths of By-the-Way. I can just imagine returning to find a 'by-the-way-she's-gone' in her place.

Returning to the room, we find a man standing near the window with a dirty cloth hanging limply from his hand. Interrupted, he turns to us and lets out an indecipherable grunt. I scan the room quickly and ask him sharply, 'What are you doing?'

'I was going to do the windows for ya.'

'They look clean enough.'

'Right, so; I'll do them when ye're gone, then.'

'That would be a better time to do it,' I say firmly while eyeing him closely, letting him know I am on to him.

'Right, then. I'll be off, so.' And he leaves.

Nothing is out of place, except that someone with a key came and went at will. Sure, what is the point of me having a key?

Tonight I'll gather up the teapot, cups, saucers, cutlery and anything else that will make an almighty clatter and crash if it falls. I'll stack them at the crack of the door, a totem pole piled high, and balance them with just enough stability to stay as they are. Then, if anything attempts to enter through the door in the night, they will all come crashing down and wake us.

✳

There is nowhere for Sugar Pea to sit without her chair. I'll have to prop her up with cushions against the headboard when she needs to be fed. I clear a space on the floor in front of the bay window and spread a blanket out for her. Unable to find her a bottle, I take a drink of cold water from the jug and carry it to her in my mouth. Pressing my lips to hers, I release it gradually into her mouth. She accepts it with ease.

The sea comes in, in short frothy waves, over the pebbles of blue and salmon-pink and slate-grey. The sea is relentless; it just keeps on coming in, no matter what. Faint voices approach, in step, along the shore. They remind me of once when I sat in Mrs Scott's cottage, at the edge of my old town, as a child – how still it was. I imagine she sits there a lot, an old lady on her own, listening to the dust and the odd voice approaching from along the southeast wall and fading away to the other side. I stand until my lower back gives out; then I lie down on the blanket beside Sugar Pea. She examines her hands as they dance slowly through the air above her face. The ceiling is smooth; the cornice is ornately carved, but the pattern in the plaster is not recognisable. Layers and layers of paint have blotted it out, clogging up the detail.

And, as often happens with bed-and-breakfasts, many of its face-lifts were only partial and so the history manages to seep through. The room has too many patterns, flowers, stripes and diamonds, all competing with the same vigour, so that no one can be heard above the others. They fight so fiercely that only the physical lines of the bed, dresser and windows stand out and define the areas. Only an edge tells you where one thing finishes and another begins.

Turning my ear to the ground, I listen to the floor through the blanket, but it's the same as the patterns: so many footsteps have passed here from the bed to the window that I can't hear a single one. All the voices captured by the beds and walls have become one, a monotone sound, evenly humming in my ears. The sound of the ocean. The sound when you submerge your head in the bath. We lie there, me being still and Sugar Pea in perpetual motion, until it grows dark and reaches the stage where I absolutely must get up and feed her because it wouldn't be fair to leave her any longer.

There is no Open University here; there are only four stations, and BBC2 is not one of them. No stereo and no books. There are a few things I want to check up on, but I have no pressing leads to anywhere. Maybe I don't need any more. I'm afraid to even think about it. I haven't seen Sugar Pea jump since we left Kilreadon. There are no more appointments, no more Gráinne. I should have left her a message. I'll send one to her and one to Carol and Matt. How easy it is to not be missed. I am more like Betty than I thought.

I am restless and jittery. Something is coming. I cannot reason away this great sense of urgency within me. I feel the clouds blacken and roar with doom as they rumble forward towards us.

At first sight it appears to be a seal, swimming directly towards us. You can just make out a darkish head with two great black eyes, bobbing in and out of the water. The oddest thing is that it's heading in a straight line for us. We were sitting side by side, me on a bench and Sugar Pea in her chair, watching the waves land, when I spotted what started as a black dot way off in the distance. I would never have thought that a seal would swim in a straight line towards the shore. It seems unnatural.

It's only when it has completely confounded me that it suddenly stands up and turns into a woman with short dark hair and a pair of large black goggles. She continues in a straight line and walks right out of the sea. Without a pause, she marches up the beach and stops just three feet to our right, where she bends down and retrieves a plastic bag from under a loose step of the kiosk that no longer functions as a kiosk.

'Hello,' she says loudly and brightly, as she begins drying herself vigorously, shaking her wet head. She looks athletic and I guess she is in her late fifties. She must swim all year long, to be swimming on a day like today in cold November.

'Hello,' I reply, still in disbelief that she came out of the sea.

'She's a fine-looking girl you have there,' she says, from under the towel that she's rubbing the head off herself with.

'Yes, she's great. Did you swim from England?' I ask.

'No, not today. I swam out a couple of miles, turned around, and swam back.' The towel flies off her head; she wraps it around herself and, practically in one swift movement, removes her swimsuit from under it. She sits on the end of the bench. I try not to watch as she pulls on first a vest and then an oversized sweatshirt, over the towel, and then whips the towel out from under them. She dries her toes with as much vigour as her head; the rest in between just got a quick rub. She takes care of both ends and leaves the middle to take care of itself.

'Do you bring her swimming?' she asks as she ties up her laces.

'The baby? No, she doesn't like cold water. Only warm.'

'You should get her used to it; it's good for the muscles,' she says.

'Yes, I've heard that, but any time I tried her in the pool, she screamed as though I was trying to kill her.'

'You should try the hospital pools; they're always warm, for people with injuries or disabilities. I teach kids with disabilities how to swim. What's her name?'

'Sugar Pea.'

'Sugar Pea – now there's a name for you.' She stands up and folds her towel in half, then puts her swimsuit and goggles on it and rolls it up like a Swiss roll with a swimwear filling. Then she combs her hair. People of a certain age do whatever they want. They don't mind just standing in front of you and giving you a good look. It's like they've earned the right to do whatever the hell they feel like.

'Do you use Respite or any of the development centres at all?' she asks.

'No. Sure, she's too young to leave. She's only a baby.'

'Well, don't leave it too long, because it'll only get harder to leave her. I've seen it happen.'

I don't say anything; I just take it in. She gives me a good look in the face.

'And do you look after yourself?'

'I do, yes,' I reply.

'Don't forget to look after yourself; you're no good to her if you don't look after yourself.'

She picks up Sugar Pea's foot and gives it a shake, and off she goes, walking briskly down the path along the beach. I watch her up to the point where she disappears as the beach wraps around the town. It bends back into view in the distance, where the green blot of land juts into the sea.

The dining room has twenty tables that fit in neatly if no one pulls out a chair and sits down. Sugar Pea and I take a table for two. As soon as I sit down with the menu, I am sorry I'm here at all. I should have got a sandwich and brought it to our room. Now that I am sitting, I can't stand up and walk out, being the only customer in the place.

One vacant fish-eye views the world from my plate. Its silver scales, now blistered with heat, have come to a halt beside my salad. It must have fallen from the sky to the sea; it's too silvery to be an ordinary mackerel.

> *'I wish, I wish*
> *On a big-bottomed dish*
> *Of silver fish,'*
> *Said the star*
> *From afar,*
> *When it saw the Earth*
> *Swim by.*

I ask you, fish, before I bite you, tell me what you know. I ask the question aloud inside my head and send it straight to him. He doesn't reply. I threaten him with a fork-prod in the belly. *Where is my father? Is he like the father in* Fiddler on the Roof?

The fish does not respond to threats; moving within himself, he changes eye and looks out the one facing the plate. I stab him in the belly and cut out a bite-size chunk; he doesn't flinch. I chew the flesh and wait for thoughts of other places, but nothing comes. I tuck a piece in Sugar Pea's cheek, as she sits in her buggy jammed between two tables, and look for changes on her face. She likes the taste. Nothing; it must have been an ordinary fish. If I believed in magic fish, I would have to believe in God, I would have to believe I could do anything, even fly.

I broke my arm when I was nine years old to avoid kissing a boy who didn't appeal to me. He was unprepared for the lengths I was willing to go to. I had always been strong for my age and size. I still am. Only a few years back, I beat a butch woman at arm-wrestling when she challenged me in a nightclub. She had mistaken me for a girly sort of woman because I was wearing a skirt and heels.

This boy wanting a kiss was bigger and stronger and un-appealing. It was outside school hours and a thin strip of trees lined the playground. I climbed up the nearest tree that lent itself to climbing, and he climbed up after me. I climbed higher but still he followed, laughing. I reached the highest branch; there was no place else to go, so I started to climb outwards. He settled himself in wait at the base of the branch.

'I won't let you pass till you kiss me,' he said.

I could have tried to out-wait him. It was much too high to jump.

'I'm not going to let you go,' he said, enjoying his position of power on the tree.

I looked down at the speckles of autumn oak leaves and the bare roots breaking through the earth. They looked so far away, and all around there was no one to be seen, other than Mary Fox, and she was too small and stupid to do anything.

'There's no way out,' he said, with a satisfied grin on his face.

He had no idea how far I would go. I turned to him, raised one eyebrow and smiled. There was always a way out. I released my firmly gripping hands, raising them in the air, and leapt like a flying squirrel. I flew through the air; when the ground came to meet me, it was my arm that hit the Earth first, and it snapped. But I got up and ran, and he never saw the tears bursting from my eyes.

When you're flying through the air or jumping out of a tree, the Earth pulls you to it; but you also pull the Earth the tiniest amount towards yourself. You move a lot more than the planet does because it's so much bigger than you are. It's good to know you have an influence on it, all the same.

*

Sugar Pea freezes for a second and then trembles. If I don't see it, it's not there. I turn my head quickly. I look back. She is still. Doesn't count: I didn't see it. We still have hope. We found the solution. The solution was to get out, and we did. Now it's over.

Pretending to tie my laceless shoes, I check under the ledge to see if Ms Seal's bag is there. I wouldn't like her or anyone else to catch me poking about for it and think I am trying to steal her stuff. I just want to know if she is out in the sea, so Sugar Pea and I can wait for her and see what she has to say today. I feel she knows a lot of things I need to know.

I do try not to write people off. It's my official policy that everyone has something interesting and unique to say – although it is easier to hold this policy than it is to actually listen to people. Some people stand out, as though you were meant to meet them; as though they have some vital information meant for you. I feel Ms Seal is one of these people in my life and has more to say to me.

The bag isn't there. We sit down and wait a while. The pebbles gleam happily today. I look out for one in need. If I were a god, would I consider a pebble in need to be of enough significance to keep it in mind? Then I remember the pebble Liam left for me. It seems so long ago. Who would have thought the plan would go so far astray?

There is no sign of her coming. We leave, with the intention of coming back tomorrow.

There is something breathing on the back of my neck. I am awake. I thought I was dreaming, but I can still feel it. I feel the foul, hot breath on the bare skin of my neck.

140

I open my eyes. Sugar Pea is turned in to me and sleeping near my heart. I freeze. There is something behind me, in the dark. Then his whispers creep over my skin and down my spine.

'Shhhh, shhhh, sssleeeep, sssleeeep,' he hisses, and stifles a snigger. It's him.

'Noooo, noooo!' I jump, screaming and wildly hitting out in his direction, one hand after another. Grabbing Sugar Pea, I fly to the far end of the room and back up against the wall and switch on the light. Quickly my eyes search the room; and there he is, crouched by my pillow, where my head was just lying. His eyes gleam; he grins hideously at us, and his fingers fan out and flicker over themselves.

In an instant, he pounces off the bed, flattens himself like a cat and creeps under the door and out of the room. I can still feel his hot breath on my neck and I keep trying to wipe it away. Shivers run through me. I sit on a chair and watch the door. Sugar Pea is still sleeping, her face damp and heavy against me. Her weight slumps as she moulds herself to me. The realisation comes over me, as insidious as his breath, that it doesn't make any difference where we go – whether I sit in this chair, lie on the bed, or drive a hundred miles. He can be anywhere. How did he find us? How did he know where we are? He must have hidden in the car, in her chair, inside one of us.

Sugar Pea jumps in my arms and twists to the side. One leg stiffens out, the other draws in; her face begins to turn to one side, and her eyeballs move so far to the right that they almost disappear inside her head. She gasps in all the air, more than she can breathe, and stops as her head and her eyeballs slowly turn to the opposite side.

'Sugar Pea. Sugar Pea.' All of her body has stiffened and my hands can't move her. The blue bleeds through her face and blackens the room. There is a cessation of time.

'Sugar Pea, breathe.' I pull at her mouth, willing her to take a breath. 'Breathe, Sugar Pea, breathe!' The air is expelled forcefully out between her locked teeth, and then a great vacuum within sucks everything in.

'Breathe again, Sugar Pea. Come on, you can do it!' She breathes again, then stops; then again. One day she won't start again. I don't understand. Is he inside her? I saw him crawl out the door. His transparency has gone. He has solidified. I look at Sugar Pea. There are no scars, no punctures, no marks, no evidence of the horror.

I open my eyes. It's daylight. My body is cramped in a half-sitting position, with Sugar Pea under one arm, asleep. I do not move yet; I only move my eyes. My stomach turns over. I am still here, in this space in time. Above me, I can see sheets of gloom layering the sky. No sun or stars. There is something different in the particles of air. I have lost my feeling. I have lost my incentive. I have broken my baby.

I look for a theme underlying all the patterns in the room and the variations of sky. There is no vibrancy to the wallpaper or the off-peach sheets. It has all been dampened out by grey. I look for patterns that are not there, trying to impose a meaning on things that have no meaning. Isolation, desolation, dislocated patterns.

Reality assaults my morning eyes; it's indicated by the position of the bed. I removed all obstacles and pushed it across the well-worn path on the carpet. I pushed the head of the bed as far as possible into the bay window. From here I could see all the parts of the room clearly and at once. I stuffed the gap between the bed and the curve of the bay window with cushions. It's safest to be backed up against a wall.

Sugar Pea sleeps soundly. Would I wish her away? Do I wish she were all over? I am floating, detaching. Such a price to pay for a child of my own. I only wanted to make her happy. I didn't bargain for this at all. Shifting around, I look closely into her soft warm face. What if I gave her a real name? Is that what's wrong – or would that be the end of her? Would it be better if she didn't take another breath? Do I pray for her to live or pray for her to die? Have I asked too much of her, to live for me? It would all be over, and she wouldn't be attacked ever again.

If it had happened when she was born, I wouldn't have known her when she lost her last breath; I might have got over it. We could walk into the sea, Sugar Pea and I – walk in a straight line, directly in, without stopping, and breathe the salt water into our lungs. Let it fill our ears and carry us away. We would have no need of voices or muscles in the sea. I am out of my depth, sinking. There are no lifelines. All the lines broke up in my hands and dissolved.

I move away from Sugar Pea carefully, so as not to wake her. I am not ready to take care of her yet. I stare out the window, up and down the road and across the horizon. All I can see is great expanses of grey. There's a spider on the sill. How easy it is to wipe out a spider: a bit of pressure and it's gone, that's all it takes. A voice says, *You don't love her any more,* and another says, *Don't worry, you will love her tomorrow.*

Now all the particles in the room are vibrating, visible to the human eye. A faint high-pitched shriek, like that of a screaming hare, hits my ears. This must be where the screams go. I bite my arm as hard as I can, without taking it away: proof that I'm alive.

*

There is only one place to go and that is back. If I don't go back to the nest, we will never get away from him. He will tear away at Sugar Pea until there is nothing left of her. And then he'll settle on the back of my neck forever. I have to find what it is that draws him to Sugar Pea. I have to go back and find a way to fight him.

I pack our bags and give the room a quick glance over, making sure I haven't forgotten anything. I hand over my keys and pack the car. Pushing Sugar Pea's chair, I cross the road over to the beach.

We sit on the bench, waiting, in the hope of seeing Ms Seal cutting her way through the waves and over the pebbles before we leave. We watch the sea come in; it is too cold to walk into. Respite in an ocean swell. Had it been warmer, I would have considered walking in with Sugar Pea, but it is much too cold. I refuse to be that cold, even in death. Once or twice, I think I catch sight of her, but it proves to be an illusion rather than a reality. Just because you really want or need something, that doesn't mean it's going to happen. We have been raised on a construction of lies, full of stories and movies where, if you try hard enough, go that extra mile, really put your back into it, believe with all your heart and soul in yourself and what it is you need – then the miracle will happen! You will get that thing you need, climb the highest mountain, become the president, break the world record, make your first million, beat cancer, beat poverty, justice will prevail! Bullshit. How does that explain a mother watching her child die from starvation, with no access to food and no strength left to make an attempt to get to some other place where they might have a few more resources? Is she not wishing with every particle of her being that her child will live? Is she not trying hard enough? If she is caught in Iraq in a war that she did not ask for, carried out by governments she has no control over, and has no

144

way to escape, how does that fit into a world where if you go the extra mile you will succeed?

The truth is, we have a minuscule amount of control over our lives. We live by the idea that people somehow make their own destinies and the poor are poor because they're lazier or stupider. And we judge prostitutes for being prostitutes, saying we would rather starve than do a thing like that, even though we have no idea what we would really do in the same situation. And we say things like, 'The reason why I am wealthy is because I worked, I went to university and put long hours into my career, and now I'm reaping my just rewards.' But what about all the other factors, such as having access to education, to food, having parents who encouraged you and made it seem possible to reach your goals, having been born in a developed country? Or born relatively healthy in body and mind? What about the fact of the Earth being close enough to the sun, but not too close, and the sun not exploding or imploding? And the extraordinary complexity needed just for a human being to take a breath? When you really think about life, all the so-called truths come crashing down. It's a crock of shit. We don't have any control, and life is not just or fair. It just is.

We are freezing, it's gloomy, and it's time to go. Maybe my negativity hurts Sugar Pea so much, it comes out of her in explosive expressions. I must not think negative thoughts.

An old woman wearing a red coat is hurrying towards us at a particularly slow pace. The excessive movements of her arms, twisting from side to side, absorb most of her energy. The upper half of her body battles with the lower half. It is not the athletic stride of Ms Seal. Eventually she makes it up to us and stops. She stares at Sugar Pea, hard enough to give me a shudder and make me put a protective hand on Sugar Pea's cheek. My hand says, *Don't you see how much I love her, how valuable she is, and that it's rude to stare at her?*

The woman grunts, and Sugar Pea takes her in with a sweeping glance. I sit upright, ready for the exact moment when intervention is not only justified but called for. The stout old woman looms over us and turns one eye to me. She leans forward on her stick and jabs one finger out. Her words break abruptly though the air, sounding in my eardrums. By the time I manage to attach a meaning to them, she has already trundled down the road.

'You know, you could be rid of her, if you wanted,' she said, nodding at Sugar Pea. 'No one would ever know, and they wouldn't ask, either.'

I kiss her forehead. Her teeth are clenched, her eyes wide on mine, her lips pulled back. There is no sound from her, just an endless scream from her head into mine. Boring a hole through her brow with my eyes, I will my self, my voice, to enter. *Let me in, let me in to help you. I will fight the battle in your head.*

11

Today, the world is turning blacker.

12

It flits around in my peripheral vision, always just out of sight. It's always on the fuzzy edges of dreams or slipping out of reach. It's on my breath, in my mouth, but not in words. I can feel the solution about me. Something I once remembered, some answer I used to know but have misplaced.

I woke up in the morning thinking I'd found the answers, but I hadn't. All I can remember is the trace of an overwhelming feeling of relief. I still feel the joy I felt after finding the solution, but no solution. Never the answer; it is just beyond me. I hopped out of bed, so excited to have finally come to the conclusion; and then, slowly, it came over me that I couldn't remember what it was I had found, or even be sure I had found anything at all.

It is the second day back that mirrors the first time I arrived in Kilreadon. I find it a relief to see two dead calves lying in the stream, having been flung over the bridge by someone who could think of no other way to be rid of two calf carcasses. We are home.

Their heads are together and their eyes open wide. The freezing cold water runs up to, around and between them and the shiny rounded pebbles, and then continues under the bridge that humps the road. The green, narrow-leafed foliage growing on the bank bends towards them, framing the black-and-white calves in their cold open graves. There has been no attempt to conceal them. Twins, dying together. No matter how bizarre a place may be, if it becomes your normality, it is your home.

I was born the day God died. When I opened my eyes in the baby ward, the first thing I saw was a TV, tuned between two channels. There were speckles dancing on the screen. I fixed my eyes on them. The sound whished in my ears and the speckles interfered with my eyes to such an extent that particles still dance in front of me. At the same time, in New Jersey, in the United States of America, they picked up for the first time a hiss. It was the sound of microwave radiation. It was the sound left over from the Big Bang. It was heat from the biggest explosion ever, and I could see it on the TV screen. It could be detected hissing at the exact frequencies predicted by Einstein's theory of the beginning of space and time, the beginning of everything. It warms the outer atmosphere to 2.7 degrees above absolute zero, and it is believed to be the afterglow of the Big Bang. All around are traces of the beginning; just as the patio bricks hold on to the past, space holds on to it.

The day I was born was the day it was declared: we no longer needed a god. We had proof the theory was right: a gigantic explosion out of nothing created all the matter in the universe; it expanded outwards as a hot gas, condensing in parts to form the stars and the planets. And by measuring how fast we are moving away, still expanding, we can extrapolate when it all began. It was over fifteen thousand million years ago, and its radiation is still amongst us.

We needed a god to create the universe before this, and now we don't. Matter can be created out of nothing, out of no time or space. Where does God fit into that? We no longer need him.

Sugar Pea keeps making clicking noises; she is happy to be home. This is her hometown. This piece of Earth might seem odd at times, but it is full of life, death, and every shade of colour, it is a place of happenings. Spiders make their own space outdoors. They spin their webs between one occupied space and another and live in the in-between. Some things do this, and others prefer to find existent places to live.

I stare at all of Sugar Pea's little bits for hours. Every curve leads perfectly into the next piece of her. It would be impossible to create such beauty. She is truly extraordinary, and sometimes, when I look deeply into her, a recognition comes over me and I can see myself in her. Then I am her. It is most incredible when this occurs. She pokes her tongue at me and makes a dolphin noise and then a great long yawn. I quickly inspect inside her mouth before she shuts it. I make the noise back. My numbness has gone, as I knew it would. She lies on the ground with the whole of the Earth pulling her to it, but, with the greatest of ease, I can lift her up and pull her away from the Earth. She snuggles her warm face into my neck.

*

Coming home, I pull up in the gravel drive, crunching my way back. Every fold in the bed-sheets has remained the same. All items appear to be exactly where my hand left them. In the kitchen, I break into the silence with every step. A dust bunny breezes off and swirls to the back of a table-leg. If he is here, I have no notion of how to fight him. Sugar Pea has tremors running through her. He could be the cause, but he could also be a symptom of something entirely different. He could be a scavenger that smelt her blood, heard her inward scream; a predator that spied her weakness in this terrifying world.

I clean everything. The dishwasher, washing machine and tumble-drier all work with great vigour as we prepare to create a clean sheet, to make a new mark. This time we will be more orderly and methodical and work our way through every possibility. Even the failures will be successes, leading us closer to the correct solution. There is a solution. The house is soon vibrant with winter light and restored hope. A mother does not give up easily on her child.

I open the door to the front bedroom and pull the curtains back. I let the wind in and it swirls through the room, sweeping the dead cells away. This will not be a place to harbour stale air, where things can fester and decay. Fear, like fungus spores, waits for a small bit of encouragement; then it grows wildly and rampantly overnight. Even if you kill it quickly, it can cast millions of spores in every direction. I clean the room and scatter positive brainwaves about. As I leave the room, the sun appears, and I keep the door open, only closing it before I go to bed.

Gráinne must have been mistaken about the cat. He doesn't look like a cat, anyway – not when you see his eyes, his grin. His face is more human than a cat's. You can't completely believe your senses. Everything that you are sure happened can turn out not to have happened at all. He travelled with me in my head from a dark unattended corner, from behind a sealed basement door. Who knows what to believe? One day I'll push a teacup slowly over the edge and it will float.

Despite my determined optimism, an alteration has taken place, furthering the separation between us and our surroundings. The skin of the Earth has hardened and displaced us. We are a collection of atoms too many, offsetting the balance of the environment. Before we can re-enter into a satisfactory way of being, we have to find a way to make ourselves fit in. We have to get rid of him, regardless of what he is or where he comes from.

I watch for clues, trying to make sense of all the incoming information; always keeping in mind cause and effect, stimulus and response, patterns, orders and possible signs.

I watch Michael's mouth opening and closing, making different shapes for longer than appears normal. Then I realise he is waiting for a reply.

'What did you say?' I ask.

'Have you got your candles at the ready?' Michael repeats.

'What candles?'

'For the electricity,' he says.

'What electricity?'

'Amn't I after telling ya? There'll be no electricity tonight,' he says, getting more agitated.

'Oh, I'm sorry – I'm a bit distracted. They're cutting off the electricity?'

'It'll be off from five o'clock this evening, for up to twenty-four hours, so it will. So you better have your candles at the ready,' he says.

'Thanks for the warning. I'll get some now.'

'We haven't seen you down The Slaughtered Lamb for a while.'

'No, I've been a bit busy lately, and, sure, it's hard to get a babysitter.' I always seem to forget it's better to give one excuse than two; it sounds more genuine, even if the truth is you have twenty reasons for not going.

'The mother will mind her for you, along with the boys, if ya like,' he offers, trying not to appear too eager.

'Well, Sugar Pea can be a bit complicated to look after – you know, with medication and stuff.'

'Right y'are,' he says, rocking back on his heels. Then he moves in closer and lowers his voice. 'If you're afraid of the dark, I'll come up and mind ya.'

A train roars by in a furious mood, sending angry rumbles through the earth. My feet pick up the tremors and a shudder travels up through me.

All the candles in Kilreadon are gone. Apparently, I am the only one not prepared for the coming night. I will have to make do with whatever candles I can find in the house.

Carol is busy, running around, collecting Aoife's things to bring over to her mother's. 'Why don't you come with us? Mammy has loads of room. Sure, it'd be much nicer than staying here with the whole town in the pitch-black. You know, it could easily be off till Sunday.'

'No, don't be silly, it's just going to be dark. Sure, I'll still have the heating and everything.'

'Are you sure? Mammy would be delighted to meet you. And she'd mind Sugar Pea and Aoife while we went out for a pint,' she says as she stuffs dozens of nappies into Aoife's bag. Aoife's alert eyes follow Carol wherever she moves, and when Carol nears her, her mouth smiles and makes laughing sounds. Sugar Pea in her array of straps and buckles stares off to the left, towards a plain wall and a plain door. I look away from Aoife and tickle Sugar Pea under the chin; she doesn't react. She must be tired. Carol already plays down her daughter's quickly acquired developmental achievements in front of me, and when something slips out, I smile and act as though it's great and I am so well adjusted that it doesn't bother me in the least. We pretend this unsettling part of our relationship doesn't exist. Her child is healthy, mine is not. My sister is dead, I am not. It's just the way of random events; sometimes they work for you and sometimes against.

'Have you any candles? They sold out in the shops,' I ask.

'I certainly do. Hang on, I'll get them.' She goes off to find them. I am free to have a good look at Aoife. She is a beautiful and bright-eyed baby. She picks everything up with such ease. She must have been born with easy genes, easy-peasy, go-as-you-pleasey genes.

Sugar Pea is three times her size. I touch her gently, feeling guilty for even noticing the difference. 'You're a good girl, Sugar Pea, a good girl.' Every little girl needs to be told she is a good girl at least nine times a day, along with dozens of kisses.

Carol comes in and puts a box of candles on the table in front of me. I pick them up and tell her I'll see her when she comes back. Down the drive and onto the road. Betty's husband passes me in a flash of red, reminding me once again how I passed her by because she was so different from me. I don't want to think about it. I closed the door on her red lips stretching frantically over teeth. Did I miss a vital clue in her, something in her eye? *It wasn't my fault I didn't see you. I can't do everything; I had other things on my mind.* Madness, don't knock so loudly. Can't you see I need to go inside and prepare for the night?

Dragging Sugar Pea's chair backwards through the gravel, I notice Marion's idiot husband has left his monstrous motorbike running unattended again. Then I notice the large black-and-tan dog growling at us, with his lips pulled back and a ridge of hair standing up along the length of his back. Cautiously I continue to back up to my front door. Once inside, I slam it.

I put the candles on the counter and a box of matches beside them. If I light just enough, I might not destroy my eyes reading. The ladybird clips in Sugar Pea's hair are sitting back to back, not talking to each other. I move to take one out and turn it, but I am stopped by the thought that she might appreciate them being silent. I kiss her head instead. Who knows what kind of noises go on inside her?

I was told to go in the end. You'd think I would have packed my bags and run out the door as soon as I turned eighteen, but my eighteen-year-old feet refused to move. They were unable to take a step in any direction. I looked at them: *Move, I tell you, feet. This is what we've been waiting for. Now is our chance. Run, feet, run.* They stood motionless below me, neatly squared inside the lines of a single tile on the kitchen floor.

I had lain awake so many nights thinking about how things were going to be. I was living through the now because I knew the future would come. It would all be over and everything would be all right. And now my feet refused to hear me. It had never occurred to me that I would want to stay within the lines of a kitchen tile.

'Go.' It echoed about my head, bouncing off the walls. 'Go.' It came from across the room, where it jutted out, amongst other words, from my mother's mouth. 'Go,' she said, 'go.' She had seeded the words in our family years before; she would say, 'Jean

155

is going to pack up and leave when she's eighteen. You watch and see, she'll do it.' It had been news to me that I had a leaving date, but I had not objected.

Now I was eighteen and I didn't know where to go or what to do. Now that the time was here, the whole world suddenly became an unwelcoming place. I packed my things; they were stupid things, pieces of paper with bits of words and sketches. I took a blanket I had grown accustomed to, even though it wasn't mine. It belonged to the house and this house did not belong to me. I stuffed things I had made and held on to into twenty-two little plastic bags. I rang the boy who smelt nice and asked if I could stay with him a short while. He must have wondered why it was him I rang, but he said OK, borrowed a car, and collected me and a bootful of supermarket bags, each tied in a knot.

I had no idea how to be a person, how to function in the world. I never got far. I must have sort of shut down – I can hardly remember; somehow I found myself living in No Man's Land four doors down, sinking further and further into a deep, dark, slumbering numbness, painting cracked faces of normality. Then the accident shattered through me. I woke up.

Everything shuts down at once. If it needs to be done and it requires electricity, it will have to wait. Here is a taste of life a hundred years ago. Life is affected by day and night to a much greater degree than we are used to. We are not exactly a twenty-four-hour town, but usually you can pretty much do most things at night that you do in the day, excluding things to do with shopping or the sun.

The dusk is seeping into the winter day, but a candle is not necessary yet. The feeble light it produces will not provide a sufficient influence on the twilight room. I lock the doors.

The candles are gone. I think back and retrace my footsteps, move by move, but I can't find them anywhere. Sugar Pea is waiting for her cold food but I have to find the candles before anything else. I am certain I brought the candles in and put them on the counter beside the microwave. Closing my eyes, I check my visual memory storage. The microwave was to the right of them, the block of knives was to the left, my car keys were behind them and they were in the middle of the counter. They couldn't have fallen anyplace. I must have picked them up and moved them. They must be somewhere totally stupid.

The darkness seeps in through the windows, settling uneasily in the air. I have to find the candles. I ring Carol in case I left them there. I carry the phone as I walk from room to room, looking for the candles. It rings. 'It's all right, Sugar Pea, I'll be with you in a minute.' It continues ringing. She must be gone. I begin to search through every miscellaneous drawer where a carelessly dumped candle might have ended up. It is growing darker, Carol is gone and there are no signs of life from Marion's. *It is only going to be dark,* I reassure myself, *not the end of the world.*

Crunching noises vibrate in my ears, just as I find a stub of candle in the bottom of a kitchen drawer. I freeze and listen. More crunching. I creep over to the kitchen door. The noise is coming from the front porch. I peek around the door-frame just enough to see a large, black silhouette filling the frosted glass. I suck in the dark air and a rushing sound fills my ears. *Oh, Jesus Christ.* The figure stands unmoving in the porch. *Jesus, what is it doing?* Sugar Pea is in the living room. I can't reach her without being seen. I have no idea where I left the phone.

Buzzzz. The doorbell splits the atmosphere. My heart pounds. *Go away, go away.*

'Hello, Jean – are you home?' A shout comes in through the letterbox. It sounds like Michael. *Thank God it's him.*

'Just a minute,' I call back from the kitchen. As I approach the door, I check that the silhouette is consistent with the figure I associate with Michael. It is, and I open the door.

'Hi, Michael. I'm glad to see you. I'm just after realising I have no candles.' My breath is still rapid and my senses heightened.

'Are you all right?' he asks.

'I am, yes. I'm just lacking in candles,' I say, trying to laugh.

'Well, then, I came at the right time. I thought you might need some.' He holds out his hand, and in it is a box of candles like the box Carol gave me. 'It was only after you were gone I thought to myself – sure, didn't I buy the last couple of boxes in the shop, and there'd be none left down there if you were in need of them.'

'They're for me, are they?' I ask. I am trying to figure out if I saw the candles after I locked the back door or before – and feeling guilty at the same time for wondering, as he stands in front of me offering help.

'I would have brought them down earlier, only the boys were acting up.'

'Thank you so much. I didn't fancy spending the night in the dark.' I invite him in and am guiltily relieved when he declines.

'Well, there you are, now – and if you need anything else, you know where I am.'

'Thank you, Michael; I appreciate it.'

'Right y'are. Good night, now.' He watches me closely for a moment, then leaves. I stand indecisively between needing to be cautious and being overly suspicious.

✳

Complete darkness falls. I have ten candles. I light four and use them to their best advantage, placing two over the fireplace in front of the mirror and two on the coffee table near Sugar Pea. I flip the main electricity lever down to ensure that everything doesn't suddenly come to life in the middle of the night. Checking all the locks and doors again, I pretend I'm not aware that the alarm has been disabled by the lack of power. As the thought enters my head, I tell myself that it's unlikely an intruder will chance to break in tonight.

A train roars by, shaking the house. It must be an express.

The candles flicker shadows across the page, making the letters shift. Black marks on a cream page. Once exposed to light, the squiggles leap out, enter my head and are assigned a meaning. My pupils dilate and contract, working with the ever-changing light.

The strength of an object's gravitational pull varies in accordance with its mass and distance. By multiplying their mass and dividing by the square of the distance between them, you can work out the force of gravity between two objects. This can be applied with accuracy to any two objects in the universe.

To break out of a gravitational field, one of the objects needs to be propelled at a certain speed beyond the perimeters of the force, to a point where it no longer has an influence. For an object to leave the Earth's atmosphere, the critical speed is seven miles a second until it is out of orbit. Was By-the-Way not far enough or fast enough to break free? Is it possible he travelled with us, in the car or amongst the bags? A candle goes out, then another. There isn't a lot of light-time in these candles. The strain on my eyes is tiring.

*

A dog begins barking in the distance. I look behind me, but all I can see is the blue-green grasses of the dunes. The barking thunders from behind them and I catch, in the edge of my sight, a white flower with five petals and a golden centre standing in the gleaming sand, within arm's reach.

At first, I think it was put there; flowers don't grow in sand by the sea. On closer inspection, I see it is rooted. It is a random and accidental event – a sport, a mutation, a reason for celebration. How inspirational. Without mutation, we would never have gone beyond the stage of single-celled organisms. Without the incredible diversity of random events, there would have been no Big Bang, no stardust, no evolution. There would be no us. We exist because of layer upon layer of mutations, because of nature's extraordinary propensity to spontaneously burst into endless variation.

And I realise how narrow our view is of the way we are meant to be. We are expected to lie within a certain size range and have a certain IQ level and not make strange noises in public, and we're expected to walk and talk and have children who walk and talk. And I think it's so peculiar that, if people aren't within the narrow bands, we think it's undesirable and try to fix them or hide them or terminate them, instead of accepting the chaotic and creative diversity of life. It's like a desire for a half-life instead of a whole one. But it doesn't even make sense, when so much of what we are guided by, in terms of acceptable norms, is continuously changing across time and space anyway. And who knows what we are evolving to? What direction is the right one? Can we even afford to live without the people who fall outside the narrow range of normality? Sugar Pea unfolds in her own complex way and is everything she should be. Such diversity and pattern. A whole life.

The dog's barking grows louder. Then the ferocious dog tears up over the dunes. I wake up on the sofa in time to see the last flames of the candles. It's only ten o'clock and I have only one candle left.

Sugar Pea and I climb into bed. I check the exact position of the candle and matches on the bedside table so I'll know where to find them. Testing it out through touch, I close my eyes and run my hand along the corner of the bed on the left-hand side. A few inches out stands the table, and I feel up the side of it and over the edge. Keeping my hand to the wall, I inch it forward until it meets first the matches, then the candle. Opening my eyes, I'm satisfied I'll know exactly where to find them if we should wake during the night.

I take one last look around me; everything seems to be fine. Sugar Pea is already falling into a deep sleep. Her two chubby little fists are curled under her chin and her lips, just barely parted, direct her breath gently to me.

Blowing out the candle, I put it in place. Then I pull the duvet up around my neck and pretend it's an ordinary night. All vision is gone, but my eyes will adjust in a few minutes. I tell myself to go to sleep and not wait to see if they adjust; I'm afraid they won't. I stuff the duvet up around my ears, nearly covering Sugar Pea. If there are any noises, I don't want to hear them. If only I could take her inside me.

Gripping the cold metal bed-frame, I try to sleep. Just before I fall asleep, I think I see my mother's angry face looming over me, and then it's gone.

Two thousand layers of fat caked the wall beside the cooker, building upon its grotesquely dripping form. *I didn't mean to be me. I'll hide under the table. I'll seep into the walls.* She splattered the fat, stabbing the fork into the frying-pan. Her anger mounted. One hand stabbing, the other one clenching her nails into her palm. Waiting, inching, mounting, flashing on and off. I sat still.

The plate crashed in front of me, smashing. A dried plank in the table split with tension just before it landed. *Go inside, quick, retreat; find a place where you won't feel anything.*

'What friend? You don't have any friends,' she sneered.

My throat constricted. *It's all my fault.*

'What were you doing after school?' she shouted, stabbing the air with the fork.

'I was just in the woods with a friend,' I chanced, hoping for pity.

'What friends? You don't have any bloody friends.' The fat splattered off the fork.

'I do,' I said quietly.

'Name them, then. Who is this so-called friend of yours?'

There was no friend. I shouldn't have said anything.

'You're a liar,' she bellowed. 'You don't have any friends. Why is that, Jean? Why doesn't anyone like you?' She was infuriated by the sight of me. 'It's always you, isn't it? It's always you causing all the trouble in this house. Sure, who the hell would want to be friends with you?'

I have to do better. I'll try harder. I'll be good. I'll make it go away. 'I'm sorry, Mammy.'

'No,' she bellowed, fire burning back my skin. 'No, I've had enough of you. Jesus, from the moment you were born.' Her eyes grew smaller. I was falling back into the red. The tiles swept forward from beneath my feet. Her nails flickered. Her anger mounted with greater and greater intensity. She charged in a confusion of thunderous forearms, hair, tiles, corners splitting, everything whirling around. Impact, heat – my leg, cheek, shoulder, random patterns. The angles in the room were changing. The rooms were changing. I caught sight of the corner of my bed. *It must be nearly over.* I lost my footing.

I forgot a rule. I did something wrong. I'll do better tomorrow. I moved the rope on my wrist to the side and gripped the cold iron bed-frame tightly.

The lock turned and the door jerked open. 'And if you have to piss, there's a pot to piss in.' She slammed a metal pot down beside the bed. I flinched and she left. *Someday I'll be big.*

13

The more you don't want to wake up during the night, the more likely it is you will. As soon as I open my eyes I know exactly what the situation is. I can feel Sugar Pea against me and I trace blindly up her back, sweeping my hand over her head and down the side of her face. Her breath is warm and even. Gently I edge my finger up to her eyes and over her lids. They are closed without a flutter. She is asleep.

With one hand, I feel my way to the edge of the bed. My heart begins to beat faster as I reach out into the empty space, whispering, 'Let it be there.' Finding the table, my first finger touches the candle and grasps it before I can knock it over and lose it. The matches are there. Holding them all firmly, I strike a match. It lights first time and flares a quick view of the room. No one is standing at the end of the bed.

What do I do, now that I'm awake with one candle left and only an hour and a half of light left in it? The electric alarm clock is incapable of giving any indication of the time. The room is stiller than usual and the silence is thick and uncomforting. The walls are blank, the corners empty. The blinds are down, but when the candle runs out it won't make a difference: it's a moonless sky, and there is nothing so dark as a moonless night in the country.

I should have gone with Carol. I should have booked a room in Dublin for the night and bought loads of goodies to eat and watched movies all night with Sugar Pea. *Jean, act your age, not your shoe size. The dark is just an absence of light. Everything is precisely the same; you just can't see it.* I wish it were tomorrow.

It could be that I'm not scared enough. What do I do if the candle runs out and he appears? Run off into the night with Sugar Pea, slamming into doors in our attempts to get out? Racing straight into a ditch of thorns and rats, I could disappear into a hole on the edge of existence. What would happen to Sugar Pea? Is this the crossroads I'm not ready for? I have to be here for Sugar Pea. I should have appointed a guardian. How could I not have got her a guardian? I would have taken her with me if I had known, bled to death with her rather than leave her in the clutches of life on her own. Now it's too late. Endlessness.

We have to get out. The car – the car has lights. We can just drive away. Even if we find nothing open, we can drive to a place with a light where we can park for the night, a garage with a human being attached to a telephone within screaming range. The bathroom emits a crackling noise. A distant scream passes the house. It could have been from an animal or a human, flying loosely, disconnected in the night, seeking relief from its distress. Quickly, I pull on the clothes I wore earlier. Sugar Pea can go in her pyjamas and a blanket. I open the door, crossing the hall to the kitchen while cautiously guarding the sputtering flame of the candle. Maybe if we moved away faster than the speed of sound.

Then I smell it. Something has changed. My vision is distorted. A coldness comes up through my feet. Could this be the edge of madness from which there is no return? The memories of the red stone tiles in my mother's kitchen flood through me and I can't hold them back. This can't be happening. I'm caught in a loop; the tapes are spilling out of the cabinets. That was the mistake: I shouldn't have gone out. I just wanted to be like the other kids, hanging around the shop, messing. I wanted to be one of them.

I saw my feet reach the cracked pavement and felt my fingers brush against the icy metal lamppost. I had to get home before Mammy got back. *It wasn't even worth it and now she's going to kill me.* Over the curb where the dead sky lies in a puddle. It had got dark and I hadn't noticed. I raced around to the back of the house. My heart was thumping. *Please don't let her be home yet.* The streetlight glowed over the bare, unkempt shrubs, throwing shadowy thorns across the cement, snagging at anything that dared to pass. The old wooden door with its brass handle was cold and stiff. It didn't budge; the house stood against me. *I am an intruder. I don't belong here, I don't belong anywhere. I shouldn't have gone out.* I shoved it in both directions and the door left my hand and opened.

For a fraction of a second, I hesitated, but there was no one there. As I took the first step into the scullery the walls wailed out to me; they knew what was coming. The broken stone floor shifted. *Remember when,* the corners cried out. The bar of soap sat in scum, catching the dim streetlight. *Remember when,* it said, *I scraped on your teeth and down your throat.* I pushed forward, past the jagged corner of the wall built of stone smashed down on top of stone, forcing my way through the darkness into the kitchen. Tiny streaks of red and midnight-blue whiz about and shriek. The angles of the room shift and every line is on edge.

166

Sounds fly off the wall. I hear myself when I was seven.

The oppressive air begins to wrap itself around me. Down the long, narrow hall, the living-room door stands ajar. The firelight flicks out, whipping and licking the walls and the ceiling where the paint has peeled back. *She's home.* My heart sounds loudly in my ears and a smell of nervous sweat escapes my pores. I push lightly on the door and, in its own time, it swings open. As she comes into sight, I freeze. There, hunched over the fire with her back to me, she sits. Her ears prick up on hearing me; then, without a twitch of her body, she slowly turns her head. I feel my legs going and a dropping inside.

Jean, get a grip, I tell myself. *You're not back there. You are in your own kitchen in Sunshine House. That was the past. This is now.* I smack my arms and thighs to bring myself back. They are solid. These are my adult clothes. I am an adult. I've grown up. Now is not the time to lose my grip. I have to get Sugar Pea and get out. Forcing my way through the dark madness, I focus on the keys. I have to get through this. I can do it. All I have to do is grab her and run. We can run forever if we have to.

The terror stops me dead when I see the space between the microwave and the block of knives. The keys are gone. In an instant the bedroom door slams shut; I jump and the candle flies up out of my hand across the room, landing on the floor, flickering madly as it rolls over and over, then out.

Frozen with fear, I try to focus all of my attention on getting the candle back; I can't see in the dark. It must have been the wind. I move a few feet forward to where it first landed and, with both arms stretched out, quickly feel around for it, but all I can find are the cold, still tiles. It has to be here somewhere. I feel up to the wall. I can't find the candle. I don't have time for this. I have to get Sugar Pea.

Working my way along the wall, I find the open door and line myself up with where I imagine the bedroom door should be, just three feet in front of me. There is a persistent hiss in my ears. I can't tell if it comes from inside me or from all around me. The pressure roars against my eardrums, threatening to burst them. My centre of gravity drops, descending down my legs at a furious pace. *Hold on, Sugar Pea, I'll get you.* My outstretched arm hits the hard, flat surface of the closed bedroom door. Now the handle – this time I'll find it. I feel out to the edges of the door, from the height of my head down past my hips. I feel nothing. I try again: nothing. I panic, I try again, my terror wells up and bursts out of me in screams.

'Open the door! Open the door!' I screech, banging it with my fists. It does not open. It's not going to work. I have to get Sugar Pea. I pull back through the kitchen doorway and, in terror and panic, I charge blindly ahead and leap into the air, throwing myself at where I imagine the door to be. Something cracks in my shoulder and pain sears up my neck. My ears reverberate violently as the door crashes open and I land on the ground at the foot of the bed.

For just a moment, I am dazzled by the pain; then I feel the end of the bed against my back and realise Sugar Pea must be only a few feet away. I scramble my way up the bed, feeling in every direction, but I can't find her. A sickening fear spills through me. She's gone.

'Where are you, Sugar Pea?' I scream.

'She's in the closet in the basement,' a voice says from nowhere. This can't be happening. How can everything leap out of the past and take over? It doesn't make any sense.

'She's in the closet, Jean,' the voice says.

No, I won't listen. I left you behind. I locked you all up. You're done. You're dealt with. I have to focus on getting Sugar Pea out of here.

168

I hear Sugar Pea's smothered cry come from the distance. It's coming from the attic. I have to get her away from him. Quickly I scramble off the bed and feel along the walls to the little closet door. I fly up the stairs. Through the skylight, I can see that the light is approaching. The room is empty. She's not here. *Where is she? Oh, God, where is my baby?*

I race down the stairs as fast as I can. The door has shut. I shove it but it won't budge. With all my might, I throw my weight against it, but it doesn't move at all. *The window – I'll get out the window in the attic floor.* I run back up the stairs, trip and fall back down. As my face hits the step, I lose my breath for a moment. Then I hear her cry out. *Oh, God, she's under the stairs. She's behind the wall in the bathroom, under the stairs. He's got her.* I charge at speed back up the stairs, directly to the window. As I jump into the air, I pinch my nose, and I plunge straight through the glass. With an almighty smash as the glass breaks into thousands of fragments and flies through the air, I land on the ground in the living room. Up with lightning speed, I charge into the bathroom, straight to the wall.

Sugar Pea, I'm coming. I grab the hammer and prise the most violent planet off the wall, smashing and smashing my way through, plaster spraying out in all directions. I bash the hole large enough to stick my face through, but there isn't enough light to see where she is. Just then, her sounds escape from inside, letting me know that she's a few feet to the left. 'Sugar Pea, I'm coming,' I call out to her urgently, wanting to relieve her distress. I wallop the plasterboard haphazardly with everything I have left in me, breaking pipes open as I go. Nothing will stop me from getting to her. The boards snap and splinter, tearing apart, tearing and smashing until the opening is wide enough to get through. I dive through, scraping bits of me off the jagged edges of nails and torn metal.

169

In a frenzy, I grab Sugar Pea up to me, while the hissing roars in my ears and the dark, narrow enclosure reeks of his breath. I can feel him everywhere, all over us. My stomach sickens and I retch. The very air stings, biting from all directions. Then I see his red eyes: he is crouched in the corner. A roar rushes up inside me, bursting from my throat in an eruption: 'No, you fucker, you won't get us!'

I hurl us through the wall and out into the hall and, in one fleeting glimpse through the front-door window, I see all the lights come on in Marion's house and the red light of the motor-bike roaring in the drive. And everything up in the air falls into place. All of the questions and solutions, spinning together, land in sequence exactly where they should be.

I can feel him just behind my neck, his sharp-pointed teeth chattering in excitement. I tear down the hall, reaching my hand out; it lands directly on the door handle and pulls the door open. I grab the electricity supply lever and reef it up just before I slam the front door after us, shaking the very foundations of the house.

Time stops and waits for us as we race down through the gravel. The electricity waits one stretched-out moment. Then every light and electrical appliance in the house comes on at once, the gas hisses, the ignition clicks on.

First, all of the air is sucked out of the house and the windows implode, sending glass flying everywhere. Then Sugar Pea and I are hurled forward as gas fireballs billow out of every orifice of the house. We land in the road as the light breaks into the day. I scramble to my feet and run across the road, towards the roar of the engine. Quickly, I stuff Sugar Pea under my jumper and shove the hem into my jeans. She is entirely covered. I throw on the heavy leather jacket that lies across the seat. The helmet hangs upside down on the handlebar. No time to think of the consequences; we are getting out of here. We will fly away fast enough and far enough, we will reach the critical point of escape velocity. We will break the gravitational pull between Sugar Pea and him. *It's our moment to break free, Sugar Pea.*

Zipping the jacket up, I quickly pull on the helmet and buckle it firmly. I straddle the motorbike. My toes barely touch the ground; it is absolutely huge and weighs a ton. We need all the power we can get. I pull back the throttle, ease it off the stand, and speed out of the neighbourhood.

The unfinished motorway stretches out ahead, long clean lines out into the distance. I have no idea where we are going. There is magic in the air around us, we are invincible. We have everything to live for. I kiss Sugar Pea in my thoughts and surround her with layers of love. The engine rages forward and I hang on with all my might. We are gathering momentous speed down the motorway, and, before I can register what is happening, the motorway runs out and we are flying through the air.

I am flying through the air. Breaking gravity. The sky is so blue. I think I'm alive. *I'm so tired. I'll close my eyes just for a moment.* I see my eyelids lower, and everything turns black.

I'm shrinking. I'm smaller. I'm not big enough.

She tilts her head to one side and cocks an eyebrow up. 'What's the matter with you?' she taunts. The shadows thrown out by the fire spit and flare about her.

'I was just out for a minute. I had to borrow a book for my homework, Mammy,' I say nervously.

She doesn't move for a long moment, just stares. Then, slowly and quietly, under a trembling rage, she says, 'I want you out and I want you to go now.'

'But, Mammy...' I plead. My legs buckle: I can see that she's not going to strike me, but somehow I know this is much worse. *Why did I go out? I knew I shouldn't; it's my own fault.* I don't know what to do. Maybe if we talked about my dead sister, maybe if we talked it all out, we could fix it. The tears burst up through my throat.

'I'm sorry about my sister.'

'What are you talking about?' she asks, taken aback.

I speak with conviction, trembling; I dare to say it. 'It wasn't my fault she died.'

'What the hell are you talking about?'

'My twin. The one who died when I was born.' She just stares at me as though I am mad. 'I had a twin!' I scream.

She says nothing.

'I know I had a twin, and I don't need you to tell me.'

Her head drops and her shoulders begin to shake. An unnatural gasping noise spills from her lungs as she shakes more violently. *What have I done?* It's only when she looks up that I realise she is laughing – a wild, crazed laugh, a self-satisfied, sneering laugh that is growing more and more manic.

'What are you laughing at?' I cry desperately.

The laughter stops. 'Oh, God, it never ends. You didn't have a twin, you stupid girl. I just didn't want you because you always acted so weird. Do you understand me? You are just a weirdo.' Her mounting anger explodes and she bellows, 'You're not my child! You couldn't be! I am not your mother! I knew it from the moment I saw you!' She shouts wildly, arms flying in the air. 'Oh, they said you were mine, but I know you're not. You couldn't possibly be.'

I stand frozen.

'I always knew. I don't know who you are or what you are, but you're not mine. Always staring at me, watching everything – you nearly drove me crazy! You're some sort of curse on me. Do you understand now?' She jabs her finger towards me. 'In fact, when I first saw you, I screamed. You looked like you were deformed or something, with your hands twisted up by your face.'

'No, Mammy, please don't say that. I'll change. I'll be different. We can start again.' It's me; I am the problem. I was born the day God died. But I could change. I could be more like other people, like them. 'Please, Mammy, I'm sorry.'

'No, I've had enough of you. I can't stand it any more. I don't care where you go – get out!' She rises, moving towards me. 'Go!' she shouts. I back away as she approaches, towering, expanding, engulfing the room. I back up, further down the narrow hall. My vision is blurring; the blackness is growing. Into the kitchen.

'Go. Get out!' she bellows. The violent air sweeps through me. The sounds shift off into the distance. I am shrinking, frozen in mid-step as wash after wash of fear spills over my skin. My feet won't work. I can't move away.

'GET OUT!'

Please, feet, move. Now is our chance.

And then, out of nowhere, something happens to me – the real me, the one who has grown up, who lives far away, who has a child. I see. I really see. I see the thing that will let me go forever. Something grows in me. Something grows up. I never had a twin; it has always been just me. I stare at her. She, who stole my words, rammed them back down my silenced throat, doesn't scare me any more. I hear a roar, and out of my throat it erupts. 'I can see through you! You're not even real! You're over! You're nothing! You're gone!'

And she is gone. She is only a memory. Now is not then.

'Jean!'

I open my eyes. Everything hurts. I can't make sense of it. All these things are moving about, vibrating; I have no idea what they mean. I can't seem to think in order. Nothing makes sense. I close my eyes.

'Jean!'

The owl is looking at me, talking to me.

'Jean,' it says. Owls don't talk. 'Jean, you just had an accident. You're OK. Sugar Pea is OK.' The owl is wearing glasses; how strange. 'Jean, can you hear me? Do you understand?' the owl questions me, while it slowly metamorphoses into a woman wearing very large glasses.

'Can you speak?' she asks. She's starting to look like Gráinne.

I open my mouth, but a sound I do not recognise comes out. The image of Sugar Pea hits me with such urgency that my voice erupts brokenly: 'Sugar Pea?'

'She's OK, Jean, she's OK.'

'Sugar Pea?' I search Gráinne's face for clues and drag myself through to complete consciousness. Her face is full of kindness. I want my baby.

'It's all right, Jean – she's here beside you. You had an accident and we're on the side of the road. An ambulance is coming, but you're all right. You're both fine. You're safe.'

'Sugar Pea?' I feel Sugar Pea moving, and Gráinne pulls her closer to my face so I can see her – only I can't really see her, because my eyes are flooding with tears and wedges of sobs are filling my throat as I try to speak. 'I was trying to get away – get away from everything – from everything that happened before.'

'Shhh, it's OK, pet, I know, I know,' Gráinne says, holding on to us. 'It's over now.'

'I've been trying and trying to get away,' I sob.

'I know, Jean. Sure, it was written all over you. You don't have to keep trying. You and Sugar Pea are fine.'

'I've been fighting for so long...'

'I know.'

I rub my face into Sugar Pea and we breathe each other in. I whisper into the warmth of her ear, 'Sugar Pea, you saved me.'

14

It isn't until much later that I am able to attach a meaning, an emotion, to the scenes playing repeatedly in my head. Reel after reel, the visions, sounds and emotions come in disconnectedly. They tumble out of cabinets and drawers and spill into an increasingly large pile in the middle of my head. I pick them out one after another, analyse them so that I can understand them and permanently slot them away into their appropriate categories.

Sugar Pea and I have tumbled out of the loop. It is a painful thing for me to realise that I will never really know where I came from. I think of my mother, the woman rummaging through the cushions in the shop. I never noticed before how small and round she is. When did she shrink? When did I grow taller? She once stood tall and beautiful. I've seen the photographs. She could have been someone wonderful. I wasn't what she expected, not one of the children she had envisioned when she was a lonely little girl. I was too different from her, the cuckoo who stared at the sky too long, who said the wrong thing in company and made odd noises. It seems to me that when someone is too different from us we find it harder to empathise, the oh-but-that's-understandable thins out and we judge them more harshly.

But then, there is no real reason for me to think that I would have behaved any differently if I was actually her, with all the various events that acted upon and from within her. It might even be that she didn't want me to turn into herself, her real self hidden inside, and I was too close to the bone, more than she could bear. There is no way of telling; so many things come together – learned patterns of aggression, lack of control and, of course, proximity. To her they amounted to necessary and sufficient causes to behave the way she did. Most of the anger is gone now, leaving only sadness. I hope she finds her way out of it before she leaves this planet. For me, I can know it wasn't my fault; it's just the way it was. It will continue to have its effects all my life. I am, after all, a product of my past, amongst other things. Perhaps I was shown the mercy of silver fish swimming near to my skin.

It is less painful to change, in the end, than to remain the same. From the tangles, knotted with causes and effects, actions and reactions and development shaped by environment, I attempt to extract myself – a self that truly belongs to me. Parts of me are no longer necessary and disappear without effort. There is the me I always was. My over-active alarm responses are still intact; they are hardwired in and so well established it is hard to imagine a me left if they were extracted. They require hushing with an *It's OK* at regular intervals. I can watch Sugar Pea's pale sleeping face with her dark lashes pressed lightly closed, and I can still hear her in the distance caught in a wail of despair, and I say to myself, *She's all right, Jean. She's sleeping here in front of you.* And then sometimes she has seizures, and I comfort her and remind myself of how happy she is all those other minutes of the day.

✳

I dream that I experience a direct and undeniable knowledge of God, and when I awake, I know I no longer need that answer, because I'm learning to live in this one. I am learning not to judge people so much. I am learning to give up control. I am learning to accept all of life, both outside the ranges of normality and within them. When you let go and accept, wonderful things happen, you see the world in a different way – and it doesn't mean that you don't feel the pain; you learn to feel all the parts of life and live them. I have no idea if God exists, or of the value or meaning of a living organism. No idea what we should be striving towards. If it was an easy life I wished for, then perhaps I should sleep for the entire duration. Perhaps I might as well not live it.

Everyone figures I must have panicked when the electricity came back on. It must have been the pressure, they say, living alone with the poor little child who doesn't speak and who's in a wheelchair and all. And that was why I jumped on the motorbike and took flight. She must have some fear of the dark, they say. Sure, it's no wonder she lost it.

The house appeared to be untouched, to anyone who didn't have ears for its language. The roots held fast, the windows were intact, and yet I knew an enormous explosion of change had taken place. Everything was different; there was a calmness in the walls, a warmth in the floor and dancing in the air. The whole of the universe had transformed itself from one of the infinite possibilities to another. It's not so much the things that happen, but how I see them and choose to respond, that makes all the difference. After all, anything can happen at any time, and at some stage it will.

*

Sugar Pea missed a critical stage in brain development. It should have taken place at around the three-to-four-month period, page thirty-six, but it didn't. It was a random event, a happening. I got to see inside her head alongside her neurologist. Sugar Pea didn't need a sedative to still her, because she fell asleep at just the right moment, with her little pale body settled in a blanket nest. Slowly the magnetic resonance imaging scanner passed over her. It constructed slice-images of her brain, based on the electromagnetic radiation of specific molecules in her mind. There were no symbols or words and I couldn't pick out any thought-codes, but the patterns and colours that played across the screen as she slept were remarkably beautiful.

I don't know if she will ever acquire language. Such a complicated procedure, it is, to make sense of sounds vibrating in this atmospheric world. In a world without words, there is no past, no future; there is only the now. It is a world of sensation, where the slightest communication takes a tremendous effort. She speaks with a sustained look, the lowering of her lip, a sudden stillness or holding her face up to a gentle stroke along the line of her jaw. I am learning her language, an ephemeral language that lives only in her. Sugar Pea's legs dangle limply over my arm. *I will hold you, Sugar Pea, and hold in front of you everything there is to see. I will find your words written in your brow and the whole of your life in the unfolding of your finger.*

I had dreams before that she was naked, running through the house on tippy-toes, giggling, her two little ponytails bouncing up and down on her head. I don't have these dreams any more. I like the way she is – the way she stares unblinking from point to point on my face and wakes each morning delighted to start the day, and the way all else falls away as she marvels at a pattern of paper leaves against a clear blue sky. She is a perfect little person. She is happy and she is loved. This is such an unlikely universe. Who would have thought that such a wonderful treasure would come my way as a changeling like Sugar Pea? What bargains I must have made the day that I was born.